# ANGEL FIRE

By
J.E. Taylor

JET-Fueled Fiction
Angel Fire © 2024 J.E. Taylor
2nd Edition



For additional information contact:
www.JETaylor75.com
Cover Art by Cora Graphics
www.coragraphics.it

# ANGEL FIRE

In the aftermath of his wife's death, Tom Ryan cannot breathe when his three-year-old daughter, Hannah, is out of his sight. His over protectiveness falls into the realm of paranoia, born from the fear that Lucifer is not done with him yet.

When that same apprehension manifests in his daughter, he realizes he needs to deal with his issues before his terror poisons Hannah's innocence. Just when he manages to get a grip on his separation anxiety, his worst nightmare comes to fruition.

Desperate to save Hannah from the devil's grip, Tom will do just about anything to get her back, even if it means the ultimate act of betrayal.

# Chapter 1

MY NAME IS THOMAS Patrick Ryan, and I have been mute since a psycho cut out part of my tongue when I was nine. For twenty-one years, I communicated differently than those around me. But now, because of my wife's death, I can speak.

All things considered, I'd rather be mute and still have her by my side.

Cold wraps around me as I stare at the urn in my hand, testing the weight of it. It seems way too light to contain my wife. Her spirit alone would not fit into such a tiny container, and I cannot fathom her remains reduced to the slip of nothing I held. This was all I had left.

Ashes.

Dust.

Tainted memories.

I can't seem to find the will to open the jar and drop what's left of her over the bluff and into the churning Atlantic. This was her wish. To be scattered in our backyard. In the sea we loved to play in. In the waves we loved to listen to every night.

The roar of the ocean did nothing to fill the void in my heart.

A gentle tug on my shorts lowers my gaze to the only reason I haven't planted a bullet in my brain. My daughter looks up at me with those wide, innocent eyes, and I remember why I am standing on the edge of our bluff.

With a silent nod, I find the strength I need to open the urn holding my wife's ashes, and without ceremony, dump it into the swirling wind. Behind me, in the small crowd of my family and friends paying tribute to my wife, my brother sings her favorite song. While Hallelujah isn't really a funeral song, it was her favorite, so we thought it was appropriate for this dismal day. The clarity of CJ's voice tickles my spine with chills.

The ashes swirl on the summer breeze, hanging in front of us as if Raven doesn't want to leave me, either. They condense into a brief image of her, and I stare, scanning her gray form. Before I can reach for her and pull her from the drop, she raises her arms and turns, executing the graceful dive I have seen her do a thousand times from the diving board of our old home. But I've never seen one like this. Never a final swan song.

I choke back the sob lodged in my throat, and just watch her ashen form fall. When she hits the surf, ashes scatter like the splash of the diver before settling on the water and disappearing with the next wave.

My daughter's hand wraps around mine, and I close my eyes with the contact. She gives me the purpose I need to not take a step and drop to the jagged rocks below. When I glance down at Hannah, her chin trembles and silent tears tumble down her cheeks. Her eyes are on the same spot where I had been staring. The spot where the ashes met the water. Her aura darkens, muting her normally bright colors, and I scoop her into my arms, feeling her sadness more acutely than I care to. The emptiness in the center of my chest threatens to take over my form, but I focus on my little girl, meeting her teary gaze.

CJ's voice cracks, and I finally turn, acknowledging that I am not the only one mourning my wife's death. I squint in the glow of CJ's aura. It's as bright and vibrant as the sun, outshining both his wife, Valerie's, and my business partner and best friend, Damian's. You see, my brother's aura is powered by trinity blood and angel grace. He is the only one of the group that has the distinction of having both riding their bloodstream.

Damian's is the next closest in brightness. I'm not sure if his is manufactured by the grace of three angels, or if it is because he is the son of the Archangel Gabriel. The rest of us are distant descendants, but we have enough angel blood in our systems to be considered a delicacy to Lucifer. Our blood apparently revives that fucker.

When we met Damian and his wife, Naomi, we had no clue of our roots, and we thought their triplets were the first true trinities ever born, having the blood of Gabriel, Michael and Raphael infused in their lineage. It wasn't until my brother ended up on the bad end of a deal with the devil that we found out we were also descendants of archangels.

Our mother came from two bloodlines, Raphael's and Lucifer's. CJ's father, Ty Ryan, also came from two archangel bloodlines and the combination created something the world has never seen. CJ is the first true trinity, with Raphael, Uriel, and a double dose of Lucifer in his blood, and he holds the power to destroy the universe.

As for me, I am not a trinity, even though I shared the womb with CJ. The man who sired me was not an angel descendant. I do, however, have a natural born ability to see ghosts. I'm not sure if that results from my mother's angel heritage or just a freak accident.

The rest of my supercharge came by way of a gift from CJ. He wanted to make sure the family was safe while he went off to shut down the closest devil's portal.

Lucifer got wind of the power transfer and offered me a deal, one I said no to because, in the end, my wife never would have forgiven me if I had said yes. It was because of that power transfer that my wife and daughter came into Lucifer's sights with a vengeance.

I try not to blame CJ for Raven's death, but it's there, just at the tip of my newly acquired tongue.

I scan my family. Steve and Jennifer Williams stand together on one side of my brother and Valerie. Jennifer's green eyes hit me like a shot to the heart. She and Steve raised me after my parents died, and she knows me as well as anyone here. She knows that under my cool exterior, I'm a fucking mess. But at least neither she nor Steve is privy to my dark thoughts.

I avoid looking at CJ. His voice cracked for a reason, and it wasn't because he was mourning Raven. He has a direct line into my head and I'm sure my suicidal thoughts, however brief, are what caused his perfect voice to waver.

I give a slight nod to Valerie. I'm pretty sure she heard my thoughts as well, but the devastation in her heart for losing her best friend was almost as crippling as mine. Damian and his wife Naomi flank CJ and Valerie, and their kids haven't made a peep the entire time I stood contemplating my wife's death.

My gaze falls on the children standing stoically in front of Damian and Naomi. Grace, their daughter, is close enough to CJ's newborn's car seat to slowly rock it, keeping little Alex quiet for the time being. Her eyes meet mine, and she offers me a sad smile before her gaze moves to Hannah's. The same silent communication follows, and Hannah struggles in my arms. I put her on the ground, and she crosses, letting Grace give her a heartfelt hug.

Five true trinities stand in our midst and the responsibility of keeping them safe from Lucifer's grasp weighs heavily on each and every one of us. Protecting the angel legacy is more critical now than it ever was before, because once the last angel descendant outside our town is slaughtered, York will become the final battleground.

# Chapter 2

ANOTHER DAY, ANOTHER FUNERAL, and this time Hannah can't seem to keep still. She squirms in my lap like my holding her is the ultimate offense, but at least she hasn't pitched a fit. Yet.

The Star of the Sea Catholic Church is as much of an enigma to me as it is to Hannah, but I figure I owe it to Captain O'Keefe to be at his funeral, since he was the one trying to find my wife and daughter when he was killed.

While the funeral service runs on, I try to figure out the last time I set foot in a church. I think the last time was my father's funeral when I was nine, but that was at the Congregational Church in the center of town, and it was more of a memorial service than this ultra-formal funeral procession.

I feel completely out of place in my shorts and polo shirt, but I haven't had time to get down to any of the stores in Kittery to get anything beyond what Steve brought that first night at the hospital, and I figure blood-stained jeans would have been worse than what I am wearing.

The incense tickles my nose and several times over the last few minutes; I had to press my knuckle to my nostril to contain the urge to sneeze. Hannah isn't as successful and lets out three mouse-like achoos. Her sneezes always make me smile, and this time is no different.

She is so darned cute, and so the opposite of either Raven or me. We sounded like a freight train when we sneezed, and she sounded exactly what I envisioned a tiny rodent would sound like.

I set her down on the seat next to me and trade a glance with CJ. His lips are pressed against his own smirk, but the small dimples in his cheek tell me he might lose the battle and smile. He is just as amused by Hannah's sneezes as I am.

CJ at least salvaged a pair of pants and a button-down shirt for the occasion, as did Steve next to him, making me feel much more like a slacker than I was. His lighthearted smirk faded.

"You're fine," he says, nodding toward my clothes.

Hannah wore a little sundress that Raven had packed in the overnight bag she had in the car, and I'd successfully corralled her wild hair into a single braid down her back. Just that simple task had made me feel like I could do this. I could raise my daughter without my wife by my side, and as empty as I felt, at least I had our little girl.

Fortunately, Raven had packed a few of Hannah's favorite toys and the blanket she couldn't go to sleep without, so my daughter had some of her comforts. The only other bag in the car was the one with Raven's magic crystals and potions and her spell book. It also contained her polished gems, including a handful of bloodstone pendants, which we all wore for protection from the spirit world.

Unfortunately, bloodstone will always remind me of her death.

Raw bloodstone had been the tool used to rip my wife apart from the inside out, killing her and my unborn child with it.

CJ's stare pulled my attention his way. His wide eyes told me he had been in my head for my little narrative. No one knew Raven had been pregnant, and I only found out via the police report.

"She was..." he says and stops, mindful that my daughter is sitting between us. He keeps eye contact with me.

I wrap my arm around Hannah and place a small kiss on her forehead, and my gaze never leaves CJ's.

He inhales and looks forward, blowing the breath out while he digests the new fact my silence has confirmed. His lips press together, forming a frown, and his eyelids blink more rapidly than normal. When he slides his gaze back, there are unshed tears glossing his eyes. He gives me that silent nod I am used to, his way of saying he was sorry without any words, and I acknowledge it with the same.

Both of us refocus on the front of the cathedral, and what I hope is the end of the ceremony. Officers lift the casket, and the procession begins.

The church empties from the front and by the time we get to the reception line, we are the last people left to give condolences.

I step in line behind Steve and CJ, with Hannah perched in my left arm. "I'm sorry for your loss," I say, and shake hands as I move down the line, repeating the words until I'm standing in front of Bridget O'Keefe, the captain's niece.

As the words flow from my mouth, her bloodshot hazel-eyes widen. Her aura flares with curiosity, but the darker colors inscribed already have me stepping away. I turn to O'Keefe's widow.

"Tom?" Bridget's voice pulls my gaze back to hers.

"Yeah," I say clearly, meeting her stark stare.

"I... I'm sorry for your loss, too," she says, and there is sincerity in her words that I had never expected.

I force a ghost of a smile to show my appreciation and give her a nod. "Thank you," I add, because there really isn't anything else to say.

I turn to Mrs. O'Keefe, and her gaze meets mine. She knows who I am from all my past scuffles with her husband when I was younger. From the sad expression donning her features, along with the parade of thoughts through her mind, she also knows about my loss.

Instead of shaking the hand I offer her, she wraps me in an awkward hug. No words are exchanged, but as she pulls away, I have to swallow the lump that formed in my throat, and blink away the sudden sheen covering my eyes.

I give her a nod and step away, holding Hannah closer as we head to my car. CJ and Steve are already waiting.

"Tom?" Bridget's voice calls and the fast click of her heels on pavement stops my progression. I put Hannah down and take her hand.

"Who is that?" Hannah asks as we watch Bridget dodge cars in a light jog to catch up with me.

"Someone I knew in high school." I glance down, meeting my daughter's gaze.

"Thank you for waiting," Bridget says as she approaches us. She gives Hannah a smile before looking back at me. "I have an odd question for you," she starts and shifts, looking away from me at the rest of the parking lot. "Um. Are you hiring?"

When she returns her gaze to me, I can tell she is trying to keep from fidgeting, but isn't doing a very good job of it.

"Excuse me?"

"Hiring. A job. You know?" She wrings her hands, and the breeze loosens a couple of her golden locks from the classy bun at the back of her head.

I couldn't help it, a small laugh comes out and her gaze snaps to mine.

"Look, I am very organized, and I could answer calls and do whatever paperwork is necessary." Her eyes plead with me, to the point I don't know exactly what to say.

"Do you even know what we do?" I finally ask.

"You hunt ghosts," she says in a way that leads me to believe everyone in town knows what we do. The only thing missing was a 'duh' and an eye roll.

Now I did laugh. Hannah looked up at me, and in all her innocence says, "Mommy always said you and Damian need a secretary."

Oh, great. Now my three-year-old is weighing in. Bridget smiles down at her before looking back at me.

"Let me talk to my partner," I say in more of a sigh than anything else and Bridget's aura responds, becoming much brighter than it had been before. I guess worrying about where your next meal is coming from puts a lot of dark ribbons in your aura.

"Thank you," she says, and rummages around in her purse. She finally pulls out a business card and scribbles her number on the back. "If you, or your partner, would like me to come in for an interview, please call me. I can start any time."

Out of politeness, I take the card and slip it into my pocket. When I cross the rest of the distance to where Steve and CJ are standing, I get a smirk in response.

"What did Bridget O'Keefe want?" CJ asks, jutting his chin in her direction. He knows the history as well as I do. In high school, I tagged her, along with almost anything in a skirt. I think I slept with most of the girls in the school, and they all seemed to blend into one big fuck-fest in my head. I stopped sleeping around when I started dating Tanya, and then the Windwalker got hold of her. Out of that horror show, I met Raven, and the rest was history.

"A job," I answer, and open the back door, depositing Hannah in her car seat. CJ snorts a laugh and I glance at him over the car.

His laugh fades and his eyebrows arch. "You're considering hiring her?"

"It would help to have someone answering the phones and screening the nut cases we get calls from." I say, after I get Hannah all hooked in her seat. I close her door and step to the driver's door. "Besides, she needs the money," I add with a shrug.

"She is perfectly capable of getting a job somewhere else."

"Don't be such a dick. She's not a gold digger, otherwise, she would have tried to seduce me instead of asking for a job," I say and slide into the driver's seat.

CJ leans down, looking at me through the window. "Are you sure about that?"

I bite my tongue before I tell him to fuck off, but based on the smirk he sends my way, he heard the thought as clearly as if I had said it aloud.

I didn't want to be arrogant, thinking the change in her aura had to do with anything other than a job prospect. I was also not naïve in any sense of the word. Because of my bank account balance alone, I'm sure the line of single women will start to form once the word gets out. It doesn't hurt that I'm not bad to look at, either, and that's what got me into a world of trouble in high school.

If I ever get past this hole in the center of my chest, I'm sure I won't be hurting for a date, but I can't even imagine that right now. I have no interest in anyone but my wife.

# Chapter 3

THE SHRILL RING OF my alarm reminds me that vacation is over and I crawl out of bed, heading to the bathroom to clean up before I head to the office for the first time since the end of June. As the water pelts my skin, I wonder if the cops left it a mess or not.

My computer sits idle by the front door, waiting for me to open it. I haven't had the heart to look to see if Chief Gallagher actually erased the video that the killer fed to my hard drive or not. It isn't something I want to see, and I certainly don't want Hannah finding that horrifying tape by accident.

I turn off the water and dry myself, still in a stupor, like I always am in the morning. My office attire isn't much different from what I wore to the funeral, because I haven't gone shopping yet. The idea of leaving Hannah for the time necessary to pick up an entire wardrobe just didn't settle well, and bringing a three-year-old into a department store is something akin to disaster.

The bed is a mess, and I stare at it for a moment before turning away. I never saw the benefit of making a bed. Especially since I'm just going to mess it up again tonight. I turn to leave the room and pause in the doorway, glancing over my shoulder.

Raven's Irish brogue echoes in my head, "We're civilized, Tom, not some nomads that have no appreciation for what we have. You don't like garbage piled up around the house, so I make sure the house is clean. Well, *I* hate an unmade bed, so get your fine arse over here and help me make it."

I can almost see her standing by our bed at home, with her hands on her hips and that irritated glare of hers catching mine. The memory pulls a smile to my lips, and then I remember she will never scold me about an unmade bed, ever again. Emptiness threatens to overtake me, and I sigh, turn back, and abide by the wishes of the ghost in my head.

I duck into the other bedroom in this drab cottage, wishing the rebuilding of our home could be instantaneous, and not months away from being livable. Hannah is still out, and I stare at my sleeping daughter. I doubt she is going to like me today, especially since she didn't wake to the alarm or my tooling around in the bathroom. And the office isn't exactly the playscape she is used to. But I really have no choice.

I can't bring myself to leave her with anyone else. Any time I try, I am paralyzed by the same sick fear I felt when she and Raven were missing. I don't even make it to my car without a panic attack.

When we were in the hospital, it was easier. It was a containable environment. Out here in the real world, I am terrified of her going missing, and this time, ending up dead.

I know this isn't healthy for either of us, but I am not even close to being able to cope without her in my sight. So, she's coming to work with me until I can get my shit together, or she goes off to college, whichever comes first.

I sit on the edge of her bed, and run my fingers through her knotted hair. "Sweetie-pie?"

Hannah mumbles and curls into a tight ball, rolling away from my touch.

"Come on, honey. Daddy needs to get to work."

She growls at me, glaring through her red hair. If this is what she is like at three, I am going to be in for a nightmare when she starts school.

"I'll tell you what. I'll go get our lunches ready, and you can take your time thinking about what toys you want to bring with you."

"Can I bring all of them?"

I smile at her. "You can bring whatever fits in that duffel bag over there." I point to the bag in the corner, knowing she could fit all her things and then some in it right now. Her eyes light up and I push her hair out of her face and plant a gentle kiss on her cheek. "You pack your things, and when I'm done with lunches, I'll come help you with your clothes."

She climbs out of bed and starts to pack her toys even before I hit the small hallway leading to the miniscule combination living room and kitchenette. I throw together a couple of peanut butter and Nutella sandwiches, because it's Hannah's favorite and I can't say I disagree. It's my new favorite as well. I can't understand how Raven didn't like it, but then again, she was never into sweets. Give her dark chocolate and she was happy, but she stayed away from anything else full of sugar and preservatives.

By the time I finish, Hannah drags her bag into the kitchen. I glance over at her and have to press my lips together against a laugh. She attempted to dress herself and do her own hair, and it isn't pretty.

"Did you brush your teeth?" I ask, knowing that may be the only way to get her into the bathroom where I can try to salvage her hair. Her accomplished smile drops and so does the bag in her hand before she turns and runs the short distance to the bathroom.

I wipe my hands and follow.

"Let me see if I can straighten out your hair for you," I say and grab the brush off the counter, blocking her exit. She finishes with her teeth, and I nod toward the closed toilet seat.

"But, Daddy," she starts, and I reach down and lift her up so she can see the partial ponytail sticking out at an odd angle from the side of her head.

"You did a good job. I just want to make it neater, so it lasts, okay?"

She studies the job she did and then meets my gaze with a meek nod.

"Do you want me to braid it like I did the other day?"

The smile is my answer, but she says "Yes, please," just to make sure I know she wants me to.

The other day I did the braid when her hair was wet and as I try to tame the dry curls, I find it nearly impossible, but at least what I've done to her hair looks marginally better than her attempt. Next, I eye her sundress and nightgown pants. The combination is a glaring error of colors, but they rightfully mix with her vibrant aura.

"Can we do without the pajama pants?"

"What if I need to take a nap?" she asks and puts her hands up in a shrug that seems so logical I can't argue.

"Speaking of naps, do you have your blanket?"

Her eyes widen and she runs into her room, emerging a moment later with her blanket and snuggle pillow.

"I want pancakes."

I glance at the kitchenette area and sigh. "We don't have pancakes, honey. How about some cereal instead?"

She crosses her arms and I'm not sure what to do with her grumpy glare.

"We can stop at the store on the way home and I'll get us what we need for pancakes, okay?"

My attempt to appease the oncoming tantrum worked, and she breaks out in a smile. "Pancakes later?"

I grin back at her. "Absolutely. As long as you are a good girl today. And if you are extra good, maybe I'll let you have it with Nutella."

Her eyes sparkle and my heart swells. Given what has happened to us in the last month, I would say we were coping pretty well, and right now, I feel pretty good about my chances to pull off this single dad thing.

I pick up the duffel bag with her toys, and the diaper bag that doubled as our lunch sack, and take Hannah's hand. "Ready to go to work?"

"Can I answer the phone?" she asks with such enthusiasm that I laugh.

"Maybe," I say and give her hand a squeeze. I lock the little cottage behind me and dump all our things in the passenger seat before I hook Hannah into her car seat.

Thankfully, my ride is short. Damian's car is in the driveway of the house we renovated for our offices. The view of the York River is both relaxing and exhilarating, and today there seems to be a wealth of activity on the water, and cars are lining the street already, despite the early hour.

I pull next to Damian's car and unhook Hannah, taking her hand and guiding her to the passenger side, where all our crap for the day is stowed. After shouldering the bags, including my computer, I lead Hannah to the door and hold it open for her.

I'm so focused on Hannah that when I look up into our small reception area, I freeze halfway in the door. Damian's bright aura has me squinting, but that isn't what has me at a loss.

Bridget sits in the chair at our reception desk, going over something on the computer screen with Damian.

"I figured you might not say anything to your partner, so I decided to come and introduce myself."

I guess she can accurately read the shock that slackened my jaw and has my skin tingling.

Damian straightens and gives me a shrug. "He hasn't had the chance to talk to me since your uncle's funeral," he says to smooth things over. "Miss O'Keefe seems qualified to handle receptionist duties, don't you think?"

"Hi!" Hannah announces, pulling all our attention to her.

"Um, okay," I say, and head towards my office to dump the crap I'm carrying. Hannah follows, and as soon as I have her settled in the small sitting area with her toys, I turn toward the outer room.

Bridget stands in my doorway patiently waiting for me to finish with Hannah.

"I'm sorry. I just really need a job. My aunt is selling the house and moving south, so I'm kind of in a jamb."

I don't say anything at first because Hannah is still within hearing range. Instead, I study Bridget's aura before meeting her gaze. Both her aura and thoughts are nervous and I cross my arms, raising an eyebrow.

"You didn't think I'd say anything?" I ask, because, despite her doubt in my following through, it was something I had been considering.

She shifts from foot to foot, and her gaze drops to the floor before flicking towards my daughter and then back to me. "With our past?" She stops speaking and offers me a shrug. "No. I didn't think you were going to say anything."

"Well, you didn't really give me a chance."

Her face flushes and she does that single shoulder raise, but she at least keeps eye contact. "I'm kind of desperate here," she says in barely a whisper.

"I know; you had to be to approach me. That's why I had planned on talking with Damian this morning."

"My uncle was all I had left," she says, and pain flares in her eyes, sending a dark ribbon through her aura.

"What about your parents?" The words tumble out and she just shakes her head, but the thoughts swirling in her mind give me a clear picture. They died in a horrible highway crash a few years ago.

I close my eyes and sigh, feeling her pain for a moment more before I dull the sensation and meet her gaze.

"They died," she finally forces the words out.

"I'm so sorry." I lead her out of Hannah's hearing range and into the reception area.

She sniffles and shakes her head, pulling herself together in a matter of seconds. "I'm sorry if I've made you... uncomfortable." She meets my gaze.

My irritation at her bypassing me fades, and I glance over at Damian's office. "So, it looks like my partner offered you the job."

She smiles and nods. "He said the job was mine unless you had an issue."

"Did you tell him you jumped the gun a little?" I cross my arms, putting her on the spot.

She shuffles her feet and stares at the floor, shaking her head. "I kind of told him you said I had a job, as long as it was okay with him," she says, and her eyes move to mine as she lets out a nervous laugh.

The irritation scratches at my chest. "Excuse me?"

Humility passes over her features, and she drops her gaze again.

"I can't believe you lied to get a job," I say and point at Damian's office. "I'm surprised he didn't call you out on bullshitting him."

"He didn't know."

I let out a harsh laugh. "Both Damian and I know when someone is bullshitting us."

She blinks and steps back at the anger laced into my words.

"Daddy?" Hannah's meek voice pulls my attention away from Bridget.

Her wide eyes calm the aggravation, and I point toward the back of my office. "Go play with your toys. I'll be a few more minutes."

We both watch as my daughter trades glances with each of us and then disappears back to the sitting area. I refocus on Bridget.

"She is a beautiful little girl," she says, still looking at my office doorway.

"Thank you, but we aren't discussing my daughter. We are discussing the conditions of employment."

Her gaze snaps to mine. "You're still going to hire me?"

"Under two conditions." I hold up two fingers, and she stares at them before meeting my gaze again.

"What conditions?" Her voice shivers with nerves.

"One, that you never lie to me. Ever." I glare down at her, stepping closer to intimidate her. I'm a pretty big guy, and right now I'm charged with irritation, so it works.

She just nods and shuffles a step back while tilting her head farther back to keep my gaze.

"Two, whatever you hear within these walls stays within these walls."

This time she isn't as quick to nod, and her mouth drops open a fraction. The question in her mind stalls, but then she shifts and clears her throat.

"As long as it isn't illegal," she says, jutting her chin in a challenge.

I glance over her head at Damian, who is now leaning on his doorjamb with an amused smirk.

"Define illegal," he says, and she spins at his voice.

"Drugs, tax evasion, murder," she spits out, and her hands find her hips. "Child abuse," she adds after a moment. "You know, illegal activities."

I share a glance with Damian and then focus on the naïve woman in front of me.

"Do you agree?" I ask, and she glances over her shoulder at me. She hasn't agreed yet and without the promise of confidentiality, I am not inclined to hire her.

"I'm not agreeing to keep illegal activities within these walls." She crosses her arms and turns my way.

"Do you consider killing a ghost illegal?" I ask.

Her arms fall to her side. "No."

"What about demons, or vampires?"

She takes a step back and her eyes widen as she shakes her head. "No."

"Good, then I think we are on the same page. I just need you to agree to the terms."

She blinks, glancing between the two of us. "I... I," she stutters and gulps before trying again. "I'm okay with that."

"Are you okay enough to sign a confidentiality agreement?" Damian asks, drawing her attention.

She nods and stutters out a yes.

He crosses to the cabinet, pulls out our standard confidentiality agreement that we use with all our clients, and drops it on the desk. The moment she signs, he smiles.

"Welcome to R.A. Paranormal Investigation Agency," he says and puts out his hand.

Bridget shakes it timidly and turns towards me. "You were just saying those things to scare me, weren't you?"

I smile and turn toward my office, hesitating at the door. "Just one more thing." I turn back towards her in all seriousness. "If either of us ever tells you to run, you run to where we tell you to go, like the world's on fire. No deviation, no stops, just haul ass, okay?"

She just stares at me, licks her lips, and nods. I can tell without being in her head that she is now questioning whether she really wants this job. "O... Okay," she says and slowly sits down at the desk.

I glance at my business partner. "I'm going to need that list," I say, and his response is a raised eyebrow. "I think I know one of the names, and I want to make sure my eyes weren't playing tricks on me," I add when he doesn't move.

I disappear into my office and unpack my computer on my desk. Hannah is busy with a couple of Barbie dolls and her stuffed bear, having a make-believe tea party. I can't help but smile at her innocence as she chatters away.

The moment I have dreaded for weeks is now at hand, and I drop my gaze to my computer.

"You want me to turn it on for you?" Damian asks as he strides into the room. He drops the notebook on the corner of my desk.

"Uncle Damian, do you want to join my tea party?" Hannah asks.

"Thank you, sweetheart, but I've got some work to do. Maybe next time." He glances at me and nods toward Hannah.

"I can't leave her," I mumble. He gets it as much as the rest of the family.

"Are you going to stare at a blank screen all day, or are you going to turn that thing on?" He waves toward the laptop, changing the subject.

He wasn't in the interrogation room when Chief Gallagher played the video. He doesn't know the depth of awfulness put on display for those few seconds, nor does he know what it did inside me. I just stare at him, keeping a lid on that memory and all the emotions that go along with it, but they burn through anyway.

Instead of lamenting, I flip it open like it's my worst enemy and press the on button before pushing my chair back and stepping away. I glance at Hannah, wondering if she can feel my anxiety. I know Damian can, because he swivels the laptop in his direction and starts typing.

I'm not a computer genius like he is, so when he turns it back in my direction, I'm satisfied that whatever had been on the computer is now gone. I don't need his confirmation, but he gives it anyway.

"It's clean."

"Thanks," I mutter and take a seat. Reaching for the list he put on my desk.

"How are you doing?" he asks quietly, and I squint up at him.

"As best as one would expect. At least I have her. She keeps me going," I say, focusing my gaze on my daughter. "The nightmares suck, but I'll live," I add, with what I hope is a smile.

"Your lisp seems to be clearing up," he says, leading me away from any sort of emotional outburst that he perceives might happen any minute. And he isn't wrong. I am never sure when the impact of Raven's death will hit.

"Yes. It certainly has. Now you can't poke fun at me at Thanksgiving." I purposely make my S's into a TH sound just for comic relief.

"I wouldn't count on that," he says with a laugh. He's still chuckling as he steps out of sight, leaving me with Hannah and the list of angel descendants.

# Chapter 4

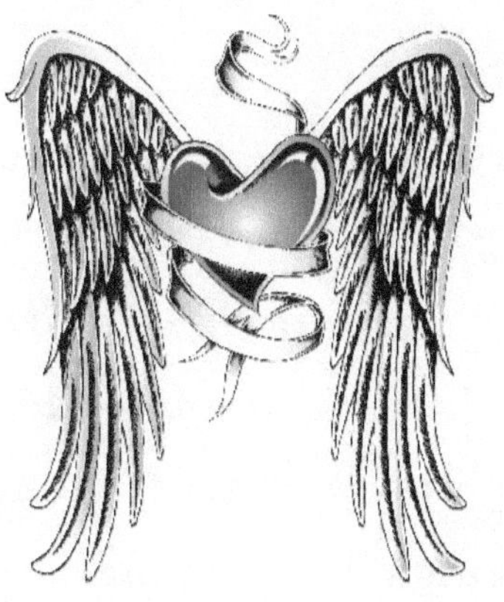

I STARE OUT THE window, with nerves bundled in my stomach, as Bridget takes Hannah for a walk to see the lobsters on the other side of the bridge so I can make a phone call. I scan my contacts, finding the number I want before pressing the call button and refocusing on my daughter.

The phone rings in my ear and just as I am going to hang up, a breathless voice announces, "Hello," on the line.

"Hello. Is Austin Shelton available?"

"Um," the female on the line says. "He's in the shower. Can I ask who is calling?"

"It's Tom Ryan."

Silence filters over the line. "Come again?" she asks.

"Tom Ryan. We met briefly in New York," I say.

"That's what I thought you said." Her voice trails off, and I get a glimpse of her frightened thoughts.

My name brings back memories she has been trying to suppress for months. "How are you, Paige?" I ask, my gaze still locked on my daughter.

"I'm... okay," she says quietly. "What kind of software are you using to talk? It sounds amazing."

I drop my gaze and huff a laugh. "Well, that's a very long story that I'll save for another time." I glance out the window again as the panic creeps in, but a sigh escapes as my senses are filled with the vision of my daughter picking up a lobster from one of the tanks. I'm stunned into silence as Bridget leans down next to her and picks one up as well. "In the meantime, I can hang on if you want to tell him I'm on the line," I say, as I notice the quiet on the phone.

"He will be out in a minute," Paige says. "How's your wife doing?" she asks with genuine curiosity.

It was a logical question... after all, both Raven and I had a great deal to do with saving her from a possessed psychopath. But it still tightened my throat. I cough and close my eyes as the pain slams home, making my chest feel like a cannon shot through it.

"Raven died recently," I answer, and despise the shaky quality of my voice. When my eyes open again, Hannah is standing on the pier holding the lobster, but staring in my direction, as if she can feel the debilitating pain radiating through my soul. She puts the lobster back and takes Bridget's hand, leading her back in this direction.

Paige is speaking, but I hardly hear her condolences over the buzzing in my ears.

"Thank you. Your thoughts and prayers are appreciated," I say as the automatic response takes over.

Hannah breaks free of Bridget and runs. She is barreling towards the house with no consideration for traffic, and that bright light of fear nips at the fog settling over me.

"Stop," I yell, putting my hand up like a traffic cop, and Hannah stops in mid stride just before she breaches the curb onto the road.

My heart thunders in my chest, and Bridget catches up to Hannah, scooping her up in her arms. I release my hold and then my focus comes back to me.

"Are you all right?" Paige is asking.

"Yes. Sorry about that. My daughter nearly ran into the road," I answer. "She is only three," I add, feeling the need to explain.

"Oh. Well, Austin is here," she says and the phone shuffles.

"Mr. Ryan?"

"Please, call me Tom." My breath is still constricted, but my chest loosens just as Bridget and Hannah step back on the property. However, the way Bridget is staring at me tells me I might have some explaining to do.

"Tom, to what do I owe the pleasure?"

I turn away from the window with no idea how I'm going to broach the subject. "Are you and Paige still in New York?"

"No. I decided Dartmouth was a safer option," he answers, and I let a sigh of relief out.

That meant the hit list wasn't as up to date as we thought. According to what the killer had on him, Austin was in New York.

"Why?"

"Because I've got some bad news."

Hannah steps into the room and stares at me the way she had in the hospital. Just a hint of worry pulls at the corners of her mouth, and she runs across the distance, grabbing my leg in a tight hug.

"What bad news?" Austin asks, his voice guarded now and his mind swirling around Hunter Garrett, the ghost that attacked Paige. CJ annihilated him just as surely as he killed the ghost of the bastard who killed Raven, so Austin had nothing to worry about from that ghost.

"It's not Hunter," I say and hear the release of the breath he was holding. If only it were, at least a ghost can be contained. "It's much worse than Hunter," I say, as I stroke my daughter's hair. "Think you can arrange a trip to York Beach so we can talk?"

"Sure. I don't start classes for another couple of weeks," he answers.

"Let me give you to my secretary. She'll give you the address of my office and some suitable places for you and Paige to stay. Your choice, it's on me."

"Sure. We still owe you and your wife dinner," he says and again that hole in my chest widens.

I can hear Paige in the background, correcting his error.

"Shit, man, I'm sorry, I didn't know," he says after a few whispered words.

"Thanks." That's all I can get out before I hand Bridget the phone. "Please find a hotel close to the beach for them and give them our address here."

Bridget takes the phone and I lean down, scooping up Hannah in my arms and giving her a bear hug. She hugs me back just as fiercely.

When I put her back down, Bridget has already left the room, and I kneel in front of Hannah. "What got into you back there?" I jut my chin towards Off the Boat Lobster across the bridge. "You know better than to run into a busy street without looking," I scold. My heart rate finally settles into a normal rhythm.

Hannah looks at the window. "I... I remembered I was too far from you," she says, and her chin trembles. When her eyes fill up with tears, I know I have gone overboard with my over protectiveness of the past few weeks into the realm of obnoxious.

I wrap my arms around her before her tears fall in earnest. "I could still see you," I whisper.

"I could see Mommy, too," she whispers back.

That hole in my chest expands, and I bite down on my lip, blinking the wetness from my eyes. A throat clears behind me, and I turn, meeting Bridget's hesitant gaze.

"Sorry for interrupting," she says and clears her throat. "But I need a credit card for The York Harbor Inn."

I nod and reach into my back pocket, pulling out my wallet and offering it to her. Her gaze is just as pained as mine feels. She takes my wallet and hustles from the room, but not before I see a tear escape from the corner of her eye.

"Hannah, baby, how much do you remember?" I ask, even though it's not something I want to know, but her memories flood my head, and I have to suck in air and close my eyes. This is the first time the memory surfaced vividly enough for me to catch, and I pray she can stuff it back down into whatever dark, subconscious box contained it.

She remembers enough to haunt her for a lifetime. I wish I had the power to erase the memories, to wipe those horrible visions from her, and take away the fear making her little body shake in my arms.

She doesn't answer me, and when I pull her away from my shoulder, her tear-stained cheeks rip another piece of my heart. She remains silent and I wipe the tears with my thumbs, giving her a small nod.

"Can you remember Mommy's laugh?" I ask, trying to get her to focus away from the memory of the machine and my wife's muffled screams.

Hannah's chin quivers again and I put my hand over her heart. "Mommy's here, in our hearts. Can you feel her?"

When she shakes her head, I try something different.

"Close your eyes," I say softly, and close my eyes along with her, pulling Hannah's most recent favorite moment into my head, offering it to my daughter. In it, Raven is laughing with me. "Can you hear her now?"

"Yes," her little voice fills my world, and I open my eyes, meeting hers.

Her arms fly around my neck, tightening. I wrap her in my arms again, wishing I could take away her pain, her loss, and let her have the carefree life she was meant to have. When her shakes subside, I realize her body is limp.

My baby girl cried herself to sleep on my shoulder.

I move her to the couch and tuck her in with her blanket and teddy bear before I step out into the reception area, fighting my own demons. Bridget stands and crosses, handing me my wallet, and without a word, she gives me a hug.

In a way, her warmth reminds me of Jennifer, and as much as I want to man up right now, I can't contain the tears. My entire body shakes with them, but no sound escapes. I accept the hug, letting her hold me together until I can collect my wits.

I finally pull away and wipe my face. "Thank you," I say with a voice gruff from tears.

"I am so sorry about her running off like that," she says, wiping the tears from her own cheeks. "Had I known…"

I shake my head. "There's no way you could have known."

"Yeah, well, I keep forgetting how much you two have lost," she says and takes another step, distancing herself from me to gain control over her emotions.

I wish taking a step back was all it took to get control over the raging storm threatening to drown me. "I wish I had the luxury of forgetting." I can't help the bitterness, and Bridget doesn't seem to mind. I stuff my wallet back into my pocket and clear my throat. "When will Austin be in town?" I ask, because I need a change of subject.

"He said he would come this weekend," Bridget says. "I have them booked at the York Harbor Inn. I figured it was the right mix of quaint, and close enough to the beach to keep them entertained."

"So is The Union Bluff," I say, thinking they might like York Village better than York Harbor.

She shakes her head. "Trust me, York Harbor Inn is more the feel you want. Besides, it's a much easier drive here than it would be from town."

She had a point.

"Thanks." I say and start to turn.

"What happened outside?" she asks before I can escape.

"I stopped Hannah from entering the street," I say with my back to her, and then I glance over my shoulder. "Anything said within these walls…"

46

"Stays within these walls," she says and nods. "Kind of like Vegas," she adds with a smile, "Or being the assistant to a police detective."

I guess working in the police station had given her some idea of the need for confidentiality.

"Yes." I debate on answering, and then sigh. "I can do... things."

"Beyond seeing ghosts?"

My lips twitched into a smile. "Yeah."

She perches on the corner of the desk, her stare now intent. "Like what?"

"Like stop small children from getting hit by cars."

"How?"

I tap my temple. "Psychic crap." I don't know any other way of putting it.

"What else?" she pushes, and her hazel eyes sparkle with contained excitement.

I study the new and vibrant covers swirling in her aura, recognizing the mix as curiosity.

"I can see auras," I say when my gaze finds hers again.

"No way?" She stands up, like I've told her I know where the pot of gold at the end of the rainbow resides. Despite being almost thirty, like me, Bridget seems to have the youthful spunk of a teenager, along with the innate inquisitiveness of a child.

"That kind of came with the tongue," I say and smile, but it feels awkward, so I just huff and offer her a shrug. I'm not sure I want to go further with this conversation.

Her eyes blink a few times and she slowly lowers herself back to the corner of the desk. "Your wife's tongue, right?"

"Ay-up," I say, shoving my hands into my pockets and half turning in her direction.

"How weird is that?"

I actually laugh. "Very fucking weird."

"I still can't get over you talking. And now this, holy cow." Her mind searches for someone she could trust enough to share this new bombshell with, because she isn't sure she can keep this juicy fact locked inside.

"And you need to keep this quiet." My sternness captures her attention, and she keeps my stare. "I can also read minds. I was dead serious when I told you both Damian and I know when someone is bullshitting us."

She let out a nervous laugh. "It's a good thing my motives aren't nefarious," she says in a way that leads me to believe maybe there was a hidden agenda after all.

"I can smell a gold digger a mile away," I say with a wicked grin, narrowing my eyes at her.

"You didn't have this in high school, did you?" she says slowly, eyeing me in a way that makes me complete my turn towards her.

My smile fades and I shake my head. "Unfortunately, no."

"If you had said yes, I was going to seriously question the accuracy of your radar."

My eyebrows rise as my skin prickles in shock. "Why?"

"Oh, come on, Tanya was all over you because of your money, and then she realized she just couldn't deal with..." Bridget presses her lips together against the rest. She would be the one person to know the real reason Tanya broke up with me. After all, she had been Tanya's best friend. Her gaze drops away. "I'm sorry, I never understood her rationale..."

"It's okay. We both know why Tanya broke up with me, and to tell you the truth, it fucked me up a little. Not as much as seeing her faceless ghost did, but..."

Bridget let out a nervous laugh and met my gaze. "You saw it, too?"

"It?"

"Tanya without a face," she whispers and glances over my shoulder towards my office before meeting my gaze again.

I stare at her, unable to speak. Instead, I search her aura, her face and the depth of her eyes, pushing myself into her head just enough to retrieve the memory. "Did you know I was innocent?"

Bridget drops her gaze to the ground. "I didn't know what to think," she admits. "The last time I saw her, she was getting into your car," she adds and shrugs, forcing her gaze back to mine. "Besides, the ghost didn't speak. She just appeared the night she was killed, and it freaked the hell out of me."

I let out a harsh laugh. "Yeah, imagine what seeing her like that for real did to me." I shift because this is the last thing I want to talk about, especially since it would bring me right back around to Raven and slam the loss home again.

Bridget seems to sense I'm uncomfortable, and she slips off the corner of the desk, approaching me, only to stop a couple of steps away. "If you ever need an ear, I'm really good at listening," she offers in all sincerity.

I search her mind and aura for ulterior motives and find none. "How were you ever friends with Tanya?" The question blurts from my mouth before I can stop it.

"We basically grew up next door to each other, and I kind of rode the popularity wave on her skirts," she says and her cheeks color with embarrassment. "She wasn't a nice person either, but I didn't have a prayer on my own. I'm too... different, and would probably have been just as shunned as your wife was, had I not been a part of the 'in' crowd." She makes finger quotes when she says in, and I smile, knowing just how desperate I was to be a part of that crowd as well.

"I guess it had its benefits," I say, shifting and looking at my feet.

"I guess it would, if you were the class slut..."

I raise my gaze to hers and catch the smirk. Her thoughts drift in that direction before she scolds herself, bringing her back to the more professional office demeanor.

"If I recall correctly, you didn't seem to have an issue sampling those benefits." I can't help the velvet purr in my voice, and Bridget actually laughs aloud.

"I wouldn't trust my recollection. It's been a while, tiger," she teases, and slaps me on the chest before retreating to her desk, but her thoughts linger for longer than appropriate.

Heat fills my cheeks and I shift. "I'm sorry for being such a jackass back then," I say, and turn towards my office.

"Never said you were a jackass. I just said you were a slut," she mutters under her breath.

I stall in my doorway as a question pops into my head. "Was Tanya the only ghost you've ever seen?"

Silence answers me and I glance over my shoulder to confirm what her mind renders.

"No."

"Is that why you wanted to work here?"

She gives me a one-shoulder shrug. "It seemed like a good fit," she says after a moment.

"I'm not sure you'll feel that way in a few weeks."

She blinks at me, and her mouth drops into a little 'O'. Her mind swirls, zeroing in on my inappropriate purr before transitioning into instant dirty mode. Her lips form a secret smile and I know she's just giving me back a little of my medicine.

"Stop that," I snap and glare at her. "I'm talking about the day you find out monsters do exist."

"I'm aware they exist. One killed my best friend, and another killed my uncle," she mutters and turns toward the computer.

I refrain from correcting her, but I have a feeling I should. This was going to get complicated, and her idea of monster is going to be completely blown out of the water when she finds out Lucifer exists. But for now, I can't bring myself to burst her naïve bubble.

I glance at Damian's closed office door, wondering why he hadn't come out, and made this more awkward than it already was.

"Where's Damian?" I ask, because it is unlike him to let this kind of opportunity to yank my chain go to waste.

"He went to pick up his daughter. He said if you insist on bringing Hannah here, he'd get someone she can properly entertain herself with while you brood over the files on your desk."

"Brood?"

She smirks and nods. "He's an odd duck," she adds.

I can't help the laugh that rolls out, filling the reception area. "Oh, you have no idea," I say under my breath as I step into my office.

# Chapter 5

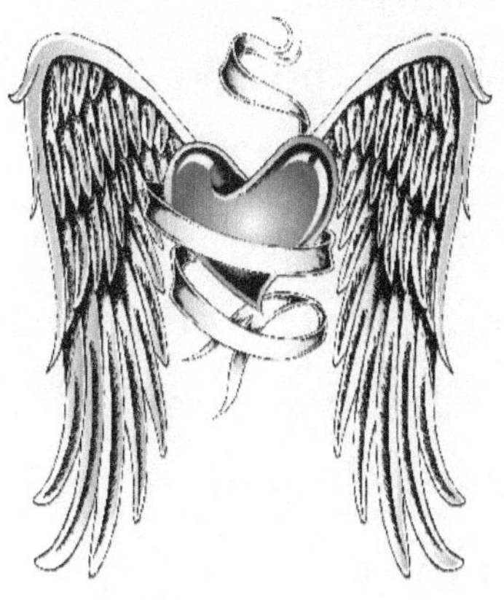

THE WEEK BLURS AND when Friday rolls around, I am more than ready for a weekend on the beach. The house construction is moving along, but it's still slow, and the little cottage is wearing thin on my nerves. At least the space at the office was more expansive. The cottage living area was smaller than my single office.

I sit at my desk while Hannah and Grace color, chattering away about CJ's son. Grace oozes adoration, and I can tell there are days she would rather stay home and dote over my brother's child than play with Hannah.

Bridget knocks on the doorframe.

"Do you have a minute?" she asks.

"Sure, come on in," I say, and she glances at the kids before stepping into the room. Her fidgety demeanor is enough to give me a clue.

"What's upstairs?" she asks and takes a seat on the other side of the desk.

"A couple of conference rooms, a storage area, and a bathroom. Why?"

She glances at her hands. "My aunt's house sold."

"Oh." I must be over-tired because I don't get the connection, and then she lifts her gaze. "Oh," I say again as her thoughts comb over me. "You need a place to stay."

"Unfortunately, yes."

"And you want to stay here?" I point to the ceiling. The stairwell leads down into the kitchenette in the back and the rooms upstairs once were bedrooms, so it's not really a farfetched idea.

"I know there is a full bath up there," she says, "but the other rooms were locked, so I didn't get to explore." Her cheeks turn red.

I let a smirk form on my lips. "Searching for skeletons in our closets?"

She laughs when my eyebrow rises.

"No, just looking around before you got in this morning. My aunt sprung the sale on me last night. I need to be out by the end of the month."

"Like, two weeks end of the month?"

"Yeah. I think that must have been what I looked like last night." She lets out a nervous laugh. "I need somewhere to stay until I can find something I can afford."

"You really want to stay in this house?"

"The commute would be easy," she says, and I can't argue with that.

"I need to talk to Damian. The house is registered under the business, and I can't make the decision without his input."

The smell of pizza precedes Damian's voice. "Did I hear my name?" he asks and steps into the doorway with three pizza boxes in his hands. Without waiting for an answer, he announces, "Lunch is served. Follow me if you want to eat!" He turns, heading toward the small kitchen at the back of the house.

The two girls run after him, and I glance at Bridget. "After you," I say, as I stand and wave towards the door. I follow, mulling over the request, glancing around at the rooms as we pass through. My office used to be the formal living area and Damian's was the dining room. The reception area is the home's atrium with a hallway that leads to the back of the house, and the kitchen, half bath, and the stairwell upstairs.

It had once been a home, but we'd turned it into a business. The upstairs bedrooms were used as our conference rooms and an empty storage area. I suppose we could move some of the crap out of what once was the master suite and let Bridget stay there.

We step into the kitchen just as Damian shovels two cheese pizza slices onto paper plates in front of the girls. He glances our way.

"You need a place to stay for a spell?" he asks Bridget as he straightens, and when she nods, he shrugs my way. "We have that storage area," he adds, and I know he's been eavesdropping on my thoughts. "Besides, if she's here, there may be less chance of another break-in."

"Wo," Bridget says with her palms in front of her. "You've had break-ins?"

"Just one," I answer, staring at Damian, weighing the benefit versus the danger. The last thing either of us wants is someone else getting hurt because of us. "But staying here could be dangerous," I add, because she has a right to know before making a decision.

She glances between the two of us. "Does this mean you're considering it?"

"It means we need to have a discussion before you go out and start decorating the space."

She actually squeals and throws her arms around my neck. She releases me just as fast, and does the same to Damian.

"Thank you, thank you, you won't regret it!"

Both of us huff a laugh at her raw enthusiasm.

"Why are you not married?" Damian asks, shaking his head in amusement.

Her smile fades away, and the silence even affects the children. What rattles through her mind echoes in mine, and my smile disappears as well.

Before any of us can speak, she slips away toward the offices.

I trade a glance with Damian and then turn, going after Bridget.

I catch her before she gets to the door, grabbing her arm and stopping her blind progression.

"He didn't know," I say, and she turns, facing me with tear-stained cheeks. "Neither did I."

"I lost everything in that accident," she whispers. "Everything," she repeats, meeting my gaze.

She'd lost more than I had, and all in one fell swoop. Her mother, her father, her husband and her child died in that car accident. She wasn't in the car because she was pregnant with her second child and prescribed bed rest. She got up to answer the door and had a miscarriage when her uncle told her the news.

I gain a new respect for the woman standing before me. I doubt I would have refrained from eating a bullet if I lost both Raven and Hannah, so in that respect, Bridget was a hell of a lot stronger than I was.

"I just need some air," she says, and another tear tumbles down her cheek. She looks down at my grip on her arm and I release her. "I'll be back in a few minutes, okay?"

I nod and let her go. She closes the door behind her, and I wander back to the kitchen where Damian and the girls are stuffing their face with pizza. I grab a slice and take a seat next to Hannah, sending her a reassuring smile.

"Where's Bri?" Hannah asks.

"Bri?"

She rolls her eyes at me and then says, "Bridge-et. She said I could call her Bri because I'm special."

"Well, Bri said she'd be right back, and when she gets here, we need to show her the room upstairs, because she's going to be living there."

"You think that's wise?" Damian asks, pulling my attention away from Hannah.

I certainly did not want to voice my first response out loud, and I just stare at him. "I'm sure it will be just fine," I finally say and dig into my pizza.

After we finish eating, and stow the remaining slices in the refrigerator, I corral Hannah back to my office for a nap while Damian takes Grace home for the afternoon. Hannah is snoring in a matter of minutes, and I open my computer to see if I have any emails.

I have a few inquiries and I sift through, reading each one as if it was real, but I usually could smell crazy, and a couple of these were whoppers; but even though I sensed bat-shit crazy, I still call to confirm, because you never know.

The last email includes an attachment and very little information. I glance at Hannah before I click. After the link is successfully scanned for any viruses and malware, a new window opens to a black screen. The noise in the background is muffled. It sounds like a busy industrial plant or garage. When the picture pops up, the vulgar display on the screen freezes me in place. I blink, trying to figure out what the hell I am looking at, and then the camera zooms out.

My legs act on their own, pushing me away from the desk with such force that I crash into the wall behind me. A laugh overlays the audio.

"Maybe this will be your daughter's fate as well," Lucifer's chilling voice radiates out of the speaker and my breath locks in my chest. I can't breathe, and my heart is pumping too hard, too loud in my ears. Tears blur my vision as the final insertion is completed on screen. Raven is whimpering under the duct tape as the bastard sews her up. I can't pull my gaze from the screen, even when she is untied and stretched out. The agony etched in her features drives pain through every fiber of my soul.

The laptop slams closed, and I look up, right into Bridget's eyes.

"What the hell were you watching?"

I still can't breathe. I can't move, but I am now aware that my entire form is shaking, rattling the chair that I am sitting in. My lungs are locked closed, and I can't even wheeze.

The concern in Bridget's face transforms to all out panic, and before I know it, she's twirled me around in the chair and does the fucking Heimlich maneuver. It forces all the air out of my lungs and finally I can draw some in, but it's now coupled with a nearly hysterical laugh.

I lean over with my elbows crossed on my knees and my forehead resting on my arms. I focus only on breathing. In, then out, rinse, repeat. It takes a good five minutes before I turn my head.

Bridget is there, concern filling every line in her face.

"Are you okay?"

I turn my head away, because I'm not sure what to say. My daughter is still snoring on the couch, and I nearly passed out from a horror-induced asthma attack because Lucifer threatened to kill my daughter the same way he killed my wife. How does one explain that to a perfect stranger?

"No. I don't think I'll ever be okay," I whisper.

"Ah, Tommy, I wish I could tell you the hurt goes away," she says as her hand slowly traces my back in a soothing pattern.

I look at her again. "You don't understand. My wife's death was calculated, and my daughter was supposed to die along with her. And that was another horrifying promise to do more harm." I sit up and point at my laptop. Anger has taken root and grown into an unmanageable tangle inside me.

Bridget sits back on her haunches, and a line of confusion deepens between her eyes.

"I don't think you want to be any part of this agency, never mind anywhere near me. I'm a death sentence. Don't you get that?"

"I call bullshit," she says, surprising me. "I used to think I was cursed. It's an excuse to curl up and die, instead of actually trying to live, which is damned hard when you've lost everything you've ever loved."

Coming from anyone else, I would have scoffed. But Bridget had lived through losing everything and come out okay, although her nemesis was a car accident, not the devil himself. I slowly sat up and glanced at Hannah before looking back at Bridget.

"You don't have all the facts and you need them before you decide if staying here is what you want. And by stay here, I don't just mean living here." I reach over to the closed notebook on the desk and hand it to her. "That's the same list the police have."

She opens the notebook, scanning the pages of names. When she comes to the page containing our names, she looks up at me.

"What is this?"

I give a sarcastic laugh. "It's Lucifer's hit list."

Her eyebrows arch. "Pardon?"

"It's a list of archangel descendants, and Lucifer wants every single name on that list dead."

Her gaze drops back to the list. "But both you and your brother are on the list," she says. Her brain isn't wrapping around the facts properly, and

I don't want to show her the horrific events that put us front and center.

"Do you get what I'm saying, Bridget?" I say and do a quick glance towards my daughter, making sure she is still asleep. "That's the devil's hit list," I hiss. "It's a no-win situation for me. Are you sure you want to be around for the fucking fallout?"

She looks at the list in her hand and then at the computer. "What was on the computer?"

"What happened to my wife in living color, and a threat to do the same to my daughter."

Bridget paled. Her gaze drops to the list, and she blinks incessantly before looking up at me. Caution paints her features, and she slowly puts the notebook on the desk. Her mind swarms with images of straightjackets and padded rooms and my jaw tightens.

"I'm not crazy."

Skepticism forms in both her mind and the corners of her mouth.

"I don't need a straightjacket or padded room," I say, mirroring her thoughts. "I just need some way to kill the devil before he kills everyone on that list."

A knock on the door and a hearty hello, interrupt our conversation.

"If you don't believe me, you can ask Austin about us. He's seen both CJ and me in action." I stand up, shaking off the horror and anger biting every inch of my skin, and step towards the reception area.

Bridget moves into the space I was about to occupy, a friendly smile plastered on her lips, belying the volatility in her aura.

"Hello, welcome to the Ryan-Andreas Paranormal Investigation Agency. I'm Bri," she sticks her hand out. "What can I do for you?" She cocks her head, studying our guests that are just a step out of sight.

A hand envelopes hers.

"Austin Shelton," he introduces. "And this is my girlfriend, Paige. We're here to see Tom Ryan. I believe we spoke on the phone," he added as his grip released hers.

I step into the doorway, sending what I hope looks like a smile, and I recognize the angelic strand weaving through Austin's aura. I'm surprised Raven never said anything about it to me, because it's clear he has angel blood coursing through his veins. Paige's aura mutates into darker shades, like this entire trip has dredged up all her horrifying memories.

"Austin, good to see you," I say, and both he and Paige jerk in place at the sound of my voice. "Transplant," I add, pointing to my mouth. "Come on in." I wave to my office space.

Their unified hesitation is warranted, and I'm glad they are cautious enough to question whether or not I am really me, because it means they will apply those same hesitations to everything around them once I explain what they are up against.

"I know this is... unusual. Just imagine how strange it feels to me."

Paige huffs a laugh and glances at Bridget. "Sorry, I hadn't heard him speak before."

Bridget sends a smile her way. "I've known him since middle school, and I never thought his voice would be so..." She trails off and I catch the blush rising in her cheeks.

So does Paige, and it seems to break the ice enough so Paige and Austin step into my office. I glance back at Bridget, and she sends a wink in my direction, coupled with a light laugh just soft enough for no one but me to catch.

"Who are you?" Hannah's sleepy voice interrupts my momentary loss of focus.

"Hannah, this is Austin Shelton and Paige Turner. Your uncle CJ and I met them when we were in New York for CJ's concert a while back. Austin, Paige, this is my daughter, Hannah."

"Hello, Hannah," Paige smiles and crosses, crouching down in front of my daughter on the couch.

Hannah glances in my direction for assurances that it's okay to talk to a stranger. I give her a nod and the worry on her face transitions into a smile.

"Hi," she says and sits up, hugging her blanket.

"Did you know your daddy saved my life?" Paige asks.

"He saved mine, too," Hannah whispers. The two of them turn their gazes in my direction.

"He's a very special man, so you need to take good care of him now that your mommy's gone. Okay?"

"Okay," Hannah replies.

The smile on my face now feels foreign and I'm not sure how to broach the subject of angel descendants and the danger they are in, with

Hannah awake. I glance towards Bridget and shift under her scrutinizing stare.

The creak of the front door draws her attention and an eyebrow arches.

CJ steps into view, meeting my gaze like it's the most natural thing in the world for him to waltz into our agency. I think he's only been here twice since he came out of the coma, so I'm just as surprised as Bridget.

"Miss O'Keefe," he says, giving her a cool nod.

"CJ," she says, opting for the less formal salutation just to be contrary.

He ignores her now that the formalities are out of the way and turns in my direction.

"Damian thought Hannah might want to come over to help Valerie with the baby for a bit," he says as he approaches the door.

"Paige, Austin, you remember my brother, don't you?" I wave towards the door and Paige flushes to the point her face turns red. Her eyes drop to the ground, and then she offers a hesitant smile. It really is amusing to see how tongue-tied people get around my brother.

"Hey," Austin says, and gives a nod, but he keeps his distance, like the affiliation with someone who can wield angel fire might toast him on the spot.

CJ gives a polite smile and returns the salutation before his gaze falls on Hannah.

"What do you say, peanut? You want to come help us out with Alex for a spell?"

I know Hannah wants to, but she looks at me with the same panicked gaze she had the other day.

"It's okay, honey. I will come get you once my meeting is over and you can choose the restaurant we go to tonight."

Her eyes light up at the bribe, and she looks at her scattered toys. Before she even asks about whether or not to pack her toys, CJ crosses and helps her put her things in the duffel bag.

I wait until she's all packed up before I step in and give her a tight hug.

"You be good for your aunt and uncle."

"I will," she says, but is still holding on like letting go would be a disaster.

"I will be fine," I whisper, and she finally loosens her grip. "And you'll be with Uncle CJ." I meet her pleading eyes, and offer the sure smile that knocks her fear down a couple of notches. She knows her uncle is unstoppable.

I hesitate before I pass her into CJ's arms, silently transmitting the latest threat from Lucifer. The tightening around his mouth and the glare that forms in his eyes is enough to settle my nerves. He gives me a reassuring nod.

"Thanks," I mutter, matching his stare and knowing nod. I don't need to tell him to keep her safe. With him, it's a given, so when they step out of sight, the panic that takes hold is tempered enough for me to breathe.

Austin watches the car pull out before turning to me.

"What happened?" he asks.

"Lucifer sent an assassin, and he followed through on an old promise."

Both their eyes widen at the drop of one of the devil's known names. Until we entered their lives, they didn't know angels existed, and now I was dropping the king of hell on them.

"And this is his global hit list," I add, and toss the notebook to him. I don't mince words, and I'm sure on some level Austin would be more prepared had I sugar coated this or danced around the entire issue. I wait while he flips through the pages and he gets to the one with his name; his gaze snaps to mine.

"What does the R stand for, next to my name?"

"Raphael."

"Raphael..." he twirls his wrist, prompting me for more.

"The archangel Raphael. The letters represent which angel blood line the person falls under."

"Your brother wasn't shitting when he said he recognized angel blood," Austin's wide eyes locked with mine. "But I still have no fucking clue what it means."

"It means you are a delicacy to the devil. Historically, he's eaten the heart of descendants just for giggles, but now he's harvesting their blood to rejuvenate himself to his former glory."

Both Paige and Austin wear a horrified stare I can relate to.

"Can I get anyone a drink?" Bridget asks from the doorway, jolting both Paige and Austin out of their shock.

"I'm fine," Austin says with little more than a glance in her direction. His gaze drops back to the pages, flipping them one by one until he comes to our page. "Damn," he mutters and glances up at me. "So, this is why you called me? To tell me I'm on the devil's hit list?"

He tosses the notebook back to me, and turns away, crossing to the window while Paige just stares at me.

"He didn't tell you?" I ask at the blatant confusion in her gaze.

"I'm not sure I follow any of this. Are you telling me Austin is a distant relative of an archangel?" Her voice rises to almost a squeak.

"Yes."

"A fucking archangel?" she asks, and her eyes widen.

Bridget is still in the doorway, and the pale shock in her features as she scans the three of us is humorous, but I can't focus on her right at the moment.

"Yes. And so are my brother and me."

She blinks and slowly sits on the couch. "That would totally explain what I saw the night you two killed Hunter's ghost."

Austin glances over his shoulder at her and then turns towards me. "So, outside of being a blood bank for Lucifer, what does having angel blood running through me do?"

"Not a whole hell of a lot," I say. "I was useless until CJ gave me a dash of his mojo."

"What makes CJ so special?" Bridget asks from the doorway, like I had been unjustly slighted in some fashion.

"He's a trinity."

Her eyes widen and her arms drop to her side. Her expression reminds me of that little meer cat in Lion King, after Simba recognizes Nala. It draws a brief smile to my lips and some much-needed humor into the conversation.

"Like... Father, Son, and Holy Ghost trinity?"

I laugh. "No. He's not a holy trinity," I say, although sometimes I wonder how deep the blood goes in him. "He's a product of three archangel bloodlines. His son, though, that's another story. Alex is something no one has ever seen. That child hosts four angel bloodlines, and if he and Grace ever hookup..." I trail off because I don't have a clue what the combination of all five archangel bloodlines would bring to the table.

Bridget jumps way ahead of me. "Revelations," she whispers reverently.

I am already shaking my head and ignoring the questions popping up in Paige and Austin's heads.

"No. Revelations will only occur if Lucifer gets hold of either Naomi or Grace. If that ever happens, then we are looking at total annihilation." I answer, and turn back to my guests. "Which is why he is systematically wiping out descendants. So, he can get back to the strength he was before Damian stole his grace."

"Who's Damian?" Austin asks.

"My business partner. Naomi and Grace are his wife and daughter, and they are on this list, too." I drop the notebook on the desk.

"So, this shit is actually real?" Bridget asks looking between me and Austin. She doesn't realize she has just voiced the common thought filling all their heads.

"Yes." I take a moment to meet each one of their questioning glares. "And both CJ and I have been..." I look up at the ceiling, trying to formulate Lucifer's proposals. "...propositioned, by Lucifer. He wants the power we wield in order to defeat Damian. We have both told him to go pound sand. So, we are at the top of his hit list."

I bite my lip for a moment.

"Raven died because I told Lucifer to fuck off."

"You can't blame yourself," Paige says from her position on the couch.

"Yes. I can. I can also blame my brother for putting us in this position. I could blame Damian for seeking us out after Lucifer tried to frame him." Hostility rises in me, coloring the edges of my vision. "I could blame a whole host of things on this moment, but it would be futile because everything is predestined."

"Bullshit." Paige stands and Austin steps closer to her. "If you believed that, why bother calling us to come here so you can give us a heads up?"

"Because I'm naïve enough to think maybe there is a way to save you." I glare at her as the words spit out.

"You know the only way to stop this," Damian interrupts, making us all jump.

I hadn't heard him come in, but I was wound up too tight to hear much of anything beyond my pounding heart.

"We need CJ to close all the fucking portals," I say.

"Yes. And Lucifer knows that's our end game. These murders... it's all a diversion. A distraction from our real purpose."

I gawk at him. "Raven wasn't just a diversion."

"No, she was payback. She was a means to tear you down to nothing, so you'd eventually say yes to his proposal." Damian glances around the room and his gaze lands on Austin. "Your evil spirit was like a child compared to Lucifer. He has an unlimited supply of things that he can send to do his dirty work. This time, it was a human assassin. Next time, it might not be human at all."

Damian's response draws a cold shiver up my spine. He turns his hard stare in my direction.

"And you are going to have to get your shit together," he says, pointing at me. Anger burns in his eyes. "You've got that little girl so freaked out that when she's away from you for more than five minutes, she has a meltdown."

Whatever fight I had in my sails dies with his admonishment. "Is Hannah okay?"

He just stares me down and then sighs. "Now she is, but it took all ten of us to calm her down. I don't have any idea how he did it, but Gabe finally got her calm. I think he might have bribed her with offering to let her choose whatever movie she wanted to watch. Christ almighty, you have got to stop this. Now."

Everyone's eyes are now on me, and I shift under the weight of Damian's words. I knew my reactions weren't healthy, but I didn't realize they were poisoning my daughter's mind as well.

My gaze falls on Bridget, and her eyes are not judgmental like the other three pairs. She witnessed Hannah's freak out first-hand earlier in the week. Bridget turns toward Damian.

"How do you know so much about this situation?" she asks, waving at me and Austin.

"Because the archangel Gabriel is my father. I'm not a distant relative like these two, and I would venture to guess that is the only reason I have survived for so long."

"I kind of feel like I stepped into a family fight where all the dirty laundry is being aired," Austin said, breaking the mounting tension.

"Welcome to the family," I add, and my attempt at humor works. Both Austin and Paige break out in a smile and Damian huffs, turning to leave.

"So, what do I do?" Austin asks, and Damian pauses.

"Honestly, outside of moving here, I have no idea." Damian answers and shrugs.

"What about magic?" Paige asks, pulling the pendant Raven had given her out from under her shirt, and both Damian and I shake our head.

"That will only protect you from being possessed. And magic is only as good as its host. Raven was a tremendously powerful witch, but she still couldn't contain Lucifer or banish him from CJ's body." Damian says and then glances towards me.

"Not even a protection spell?" Paige challenges. "I would think that would deter someone from finding us, don't you?"

"Against a human, you will probably survive. So, once you get home, it would be beneficial to enact some of that practical magic to keep you hidden from prying eyes." Damian says and turns his attention to me. "I'm going home to give CJ a break from the girls," he adds and then leaves us to continue our conversation.

"Why would moving here keep us safe?" Austin ventured.

"Because Lucifer has this town tagged as the last one to hit. I'm not sure if his rationale is that he will be strong enough to take on the three of us by that time, or if he is hoping Damian and CJ will produce more trinity girls that he can enslave for his dark plan."

Quiet descends, and both Paige and Austin take a seat on the couch; unsure of what to say or do next.

"Why don't you go enjoy the rest of the afternoon," I say. "We can talk at dinner. You still have my cell number, right?"

Austin pulls the card I gave him in New York earlier this year, out of his wallet, flashing it at me. "Thanks. We've got a lot to digest."

He isn't kidding, and I'm more than aware the moment he is in a normal hotel room, all of this is going to sound insane. Hell, sometimes I question my own sanity, so I wouldn't blame him if he chalks all this up to me cracking because my wife died.

They cross and Austin offers me his hand; I shake it. Paige trades places with him and instead of shaking my hand, she wraps me in a hug. For a moment, I'm stunned by the sadness flowing from her, but I recover before she releases me, and I offer her a strained smile.

Bridget walks them out and I slump on the couch, studying my clasped hands until she steps into the office again. She approaches slowly, like I could break at any moment, and I glare up at her.

"Don't treat me like I belong in a padded room."

"Seriously? After all the shit you laid out, can you blame us?"

"Us?" I straighten.

She flicks a card at me and takes a seat on the opposite side of the couch. "It's a number for a national help line. Austin thought you might need to use it."

I let out a humorless chuckle. "Your uncle believed us," I say, keeping her gaze locked on mine.

She looks away and sighs, "Yeah, well..." She trails off and crosses to the window. Her doubts wrap around me like a hangman's noose.

"Do you need some sort of demonstration?" I ask and she turns towards me with eyebrows arched in surprise.

"That's not necessary," she says, but her curiosity is already itching to see something more than my daughter held in place by an invisible hand.

I can only think of one way to truly show her what freaks of nature we really are, and I glance at the window, willing myself to be on the other side. After a blink, the sunlight streams down, hot on my skin and I turn, glancing inside my office from the outside of the house.

Bridget is crossing the room towards my body, which is sitting in suspended animation. The glazed eyes really freak me out, but I reach up and knock on the window. When she spins toward the noise, her gaze locks with mine and she halts. Her head whips between my still form and me outside, making strands of hair fall out of her neat bun. It's quite comical, and a smirk finds my lips. That seems to jump-start her movement, and she comes to the window, opening it.

"What the fuck?"

I reach in and grab her hand, pressing it to my cheek. "I'm solid in both places." Then I step back and close my eyes, feeling the pull back into my body.

When my eyes open, her gaze locks on me, and her back presses against the window.

I lean back on the couch, taking in her horrified stare, and then look beyond her at the window. It closes at my direction. Bridget jumps away from the glass, her eyes nearly bug out of her head, and I send a cocky smile in her direction. Not only have I made her a believer without showing her the memories, I have truly freaked her out.

"So, knowing what you do now, do you really want to work here?"

Bridget takes a deep breath, quelling the fear pulsing from her, before she considers my question. My gaze never leaves hers and when she finally nods, I can't help but ask.

"Why?"

"Because my uncle told me I needed to look out for you," she says quietly.

A cold sweat passes over my skin. "Excuse me?"

"The day he died..." She stops and closes her eyes. "After he died, he came to me and said it was my job to look after you because you were going to need someone who had suffered a similar loss." Her eyes open, meeting mine. She adds a small shrug. "So, I'm kind of obligated."

Stunned doesn't describe what's happening in my mind, and my body goes numb from the shock. I take a full minute to find my voice. "So, your uncle assumed Raven and Hannah were going to die."

She lets out a little laugh. "I guess he underestimated you and your family's arsenal."

"Hannah would have died if we hadn't had some magic at our disposal," I say, but I'm not ready to disclose my sister-in-law's healing powers. I swallow and stand. "I guess you will want to see that room then."

She shifts and sighs. "If you don't mind."

Without waiting for her, I turn away and head toward the kitchen. Her footsteps follow, and I don't acknowledge her until I've unlocked the door at the end of the short upstairs hallway. The master suite is close to six hundred square feet, and as I swing the door open, to the mostly empty room, her eyes twinkle. Our storage consists of a half dozen file cabinets in the center of the room. We could easily move them to one of the conference rooms. A few empty boxes also speckled the space.

Bridget slows to a stop next to the file cabinets, her gaze locks on the river view, and then she turns back to me. "Are you serious?" she asks, waving at the ample space.

I'm not sure whether her statement is because she's upset by the accommodations or awed by it. "Um, yeah," I say, glancing around. Before I can ask if she's okay with it, she has crossed the distance and throws her arms around my neck.

"It's perfect," she says and squeezes me tighter than I think she means to.

Without thought, my hands find her waist and she pulls away, her smile fading a notch as our eyes lock. The flurry in her mind revolving around furniture and curtains, and everything else required to make the bedroom livable stalls in her mind.

I am more than aware of her heartbeat next to mine, and she licks her lips, stirring an animalistic need. I drop my hands and step back, appalled at the turn of my thoughts. Bridget is as beautiful today as she was in high school, but this is completely wrong.

Wrong time.

Wrong place.

Wrong woman.

I sidestep out of her loose grip and head to the room to our left. "There's an en suite," I say, opening the door to an ample bathroom. "I think they had just redone this before we bought the house," I add, trying to ignore the question in her gaze.

Bridget crosses and stands next to me, surveying the old claw-foot tub and the corner shower and the granite covered vanity.

"Why didn't you take this space?" she asks, glancing at me.

I look around the area and then back at her with a shrug. "It never dawned on me," I say. "And I think where we are all staying isn't a bad temporary solution. Having everyone within walking distance is good for our peace of mind right now."

She gives me a soft smile. "Are you going to move closer to your brother?" As she talks, she steps closer and I'm now aware of the attraction radiating off her. Her hand lands softly on my chest.

"What are you doing?" I ask, staring down at her.

Her eyes widen and drops to the hand pressed against my chest before she yanks it away, like I am hot enough to burn. "I... I'm sorry," she says and her cheeks bloom red. She steps away quickly.

"Just to make things perfectly clear. Nothing is going to happen here." I point between us. "You took a job with my firm, and I will *not* complicate things by sleeping with you, no matter how attractive you are. Got it?"

She crosses her arms and levels a hard glare in my direction. "Just for the record, I do not want to sleep with you."

The burn of rejection flushes my skin, and I step closer.

"Liar," I growl and march out of the room, because I know if I stay, I am going to do something I will regret.

# Chapter 6

AS SOON AS I settle into my car, guilt replaces the burn of anger.

"What the hell are you doing?" I glare at my reflection in the rearview mirror. No answer comes and I close my eyes while the air conditioner kicks in, blowing marginally cooler air on my face.

Instead of further complicating matters, I slide the car into reverse and back out of the driveway, heading toward the cottage and the remainder of the afternoon on the beach. I'm tempted to leave

Hannah with Damian and just surf my aggravation out, but I can't help the nervous itch in my core.

At the cottages, only CJ's car is there, and I cross to his door, knocking. It takes a few minutes and the door cracks open. Valerie's tired eyes look out at me. The rest of the cottage behind her is dark and quiet.

"I guess Damian picked up Hannah?" I say, keeping my voice quiet.

She nods. "They all went to the beach."

"And I just woke you, didn't I." My timing sucks and I mutter an apology and turn to leave.

"How are you doing?" she asks, stopping me.

I consider how to answer and turn back to her. I've been on autopilot taking care of Hannah for the past month, so much so that I really haven't had time to think. "I'm numb," I say and meet her gaze. "Just going through the motions for Hannah's sake," I add. "And when I'm not numb, the emptiness hurts so much I can't breathe."

She bites her lower lip, and her eyes fill with tears. "I miss her," she says.

"You and me both," I say and step closer, offering a hug because she looks like she needs it. Valerie steps into my arms and her tears dampen my shoulder. She stays there for a full minute before she pulls away and wipes her face.

"Thanks, I needed that," she says and tries on a smile. "I'm going to attempt to get a little more sleep before Alex wakes up," she adds and retreats into the cottage.

With surfing in mind, I change into my suit, grab a towel and my wallet, and head towards the surf shop. The missile destroyed all my boards and wetsuits, and it's time I replace some things.

Twenty minutes later, I'm suited up and standing on Long Sands beach, right in front of the bathhouse. The waves are decent for the southern Maine shore.

"Daddy!" Hannah's happy shriek pulls my attention and I smile as she breaks free of Naomi's hand and runs at full speed in my direction.

I lay the board down on the sand and scoop her up in my arms, twirling around with her the way she loves me to. "Hey, peanut! Mind if I go surfing for a little while?" I nod toward the waves and her smile falters.

I see the hesitation I'd built in her, and I silently curse my overprotective tendencies.

"Hannah, why don't you let your father catch a few waves while we finish building that sandcastle," Naomi says as she steps next to me. Grace pulls on her hand, trying to maneuver her towards the bathhouse, which I gather was their original intent before my daughter saw me standing here.

"That sounds like a great idea. Make sure you make a tower just for me," I say, trying not to cling too tightly. Now that she is in my arms, I don't want to let her go, but I force myself to put her on the sand next to Naomi. "I won't surf all afternoon, I promise," I say.

A part of me weeps when she takes Naomi's offered hand, and she turns away towards their destination. Instead of watching her until she is out of sight, I force myself to turn and study the waves, fighting the internal battle to just find where they are parked and hang out there all day. I need to feel something again, and that clinches my decision.

I pick up my board and choose not to harp on my daughter today. It would be healthier for both of us if I loosen the reins a little. Without over-thinking it, I head into the ocean, letting the cool Atlantic chill the burn from my body as much as from my mind. I focus on the waves and nothing else, riding them in and then dropping and paddling back out. I have no idea how long I surfed, but my legs ache in that worn out way when I finally walk back onto the sand.

I scan the beach slowly, unsure of how far the family is from the bathhouse. It takes two sweeps of the beach to find the crew. I let out a small laugh at the elaborate sandcastle in progress, wondering how the hell I missed it on my first scan.

I drop the board next to the chairs and peel off my wetsuit, laying it out on the board before I approach the intense construction.

"What are you building? The Taj Mahal?" I ask, and all eyes snap to mine.

"Daddy, it's our castle," Hannah says and wipes a stray hair from her cheek, leaving a sand streak instead. "Do you like it?"

Her eyes sparkle like I haven't seen since before Raven died, and I return her beaming smile. "I'm seriously impressed. What do you need me to do?"

She glances at the monstrosity surrounding her and then looks up at me. "Can you get us water for the moat?" she asks, pointing to one of the discarded buckets. I trade a glance with Damian and he nods towards the bucket.

"You heard the boss," he says.

I collect two buckets of water and cross the expanse of low tide beach.

"Where do you want these?" I ask, and both Hannah and Grace point to the deep gully surrounding their castle.

I pour the buckets in, and the water spreads before seeping into the sand. It isn't deep enough to hold the water until closer to high tide. I glance at my daughter, and she presses her lips together in contemplation.

"Maybe I should just watch you build?" I ask, hoping she lets me off the hook.

Her gaze moves to Grace's and then back to mine with a nod. I collapse in one of the chairs, hoping neither Damian nor Naomi are upset by my begging off. They seem to have the kids under control.

I close my eyes, letting the heat of the afternoon cancel the chill that settled into my bones from my time in the water. The chatter of the kids fades into the thoughts accosting me, and I focus on nothing until it all becomes a dull swirl in my head.

*"Tom?" her Irish lilt caresses me and I open my eyes to Raven's auburn framed face.*

*"Yeah," I say and offer a smile. The closeness of her fills my world, erasing the emptiness and leaving me longing to touch her.*

*"Ya have to let go," she whispers, her voice rides on the gentle breeze.*

*"Why?"*

*"Because if ya don't, you will become bitter and end up doing something you will live to regret."*

*"Like what?" I get lost in her deep blue eyes.*

*"Like becoming as destructive as my father... or worse."*

I sit straight up, like someone zapped me. My chest constricts with the weight of her words. I'm not sure if it was just a dream or really Raven talking to me from the great beyond, but the last thing she said strikes such fear in me that my gaze darts to Hannah.

I must not have been sleeping long because the kids are still actively discussing how to get the moat working. The only one looking directly at me is Damian, and that small crease between his eyes tells me he might have heard some of my dream, or at least feels the fear scratching every inch of my exposed skin.

I just shake my head because I really don't want to discuss this, especially not in front of my daughter. I tap my wrist and raise an eyebrow.

"It's a little after four," Damian answers my silent question.

"Thanks," I direct towards him, and then my attention shifts to Hannah. "Hey, missy, where did you want to have dinner tonight?" I ask around a yawn, and I'm really hoping it isn't McDonald's. I am in the mood for a more formal setting.

She turns and points to the Sun and Surf, which is a little over a hundred yards away. "I want to watch the castle."

"Okay. Do you mind if my friends come to dinner with us?"

Her head cocks like an intrigued puppy.

"Austin and Paige?" I clarify. "The ones who were at the office this morning?" I add when that blank look doesn't disappear.

She presses her lips together in that unhappy frown that I am getting used to.

"You can talk to Paige about her magic," I say, reaching for something to turn this around, and her head cocks farther, but interest sparks in her eyes.

"She knows magic?"

I smile and nod. "She isn't as practiced as your mother, but maybe she could teach you a few things."

The spark ignites and she grins. "Okay," she says, and goes back to carefully crafting a small path from the castle entry. "Can Bri come too?"

"She's probably busy tonight, hon," I say, avoiding saying 'hell no' out loud. I don't even want to think about how that would go down. Besides, I'm not even sure Bridget will be at the office on Monday with how we left things.

The instant scowl on Damian's face brings the guilt back full force. I should have shown more restraint with Bridget; letting her get under my skin was a mistake.

There will be no more mistakes.

Mistakes in my world mean someone dies.

# Chapter 7

I SIT WITH MY back to the ocean, leaving the stellar view for Paige and Austin when they arrive. Hannah sits next to me on the side, where she has an unobstructed view of their delightfully elaborate sandcastle. Her legs swing on the chair, and she picks at the chips I asked the waitress to bring to the table. I sip the screwdriver I ordered, and we watch the tide creep towards her masterpiece.

"Daddy, can you keep the water away from my castle?" she asks, still staring at the approaching water.

It's close to a yard away from the moat encircling the sand art and I sigh. I could keep the water away if I wanted to, but the spectacle it would create wouldn't be worth it.

Hannah glances at me when I don't answer.

"Daddy?"

"You know I can," I say under my breath and glance down at her. "But it really isn't wise to use the power for selfish reasons."

She bites her lip and turns back towards the castle.

"We took a lot of pictures," I remind her. My cell phone has close to thirty photos of Hannah, Grace, Gabe, and Michael showing off around their mighty construction, and I stopped to get a few more of just Hannah in her cute new sundress on the way to the restaurant.

Before she gives me a major three-year-old attitude, Austin and Paige are escorted to the table. They take the seats opposite us and when their gaze drops to mine, I smile.

"I figured you'd appreciate the view. Besides, munchkin here wanted to watch her sandcastle until the tide took it." I nod towards the expanse of beach on my right.

Paige's eyebrows rise. "She made that?"

"Yes. I made that with my friends," Hannah says with such pride, it brings a smile to all our faces.

"Damian and Naomi helped, too," I add, and she nods.

The waitress interrupts, and both Paige and Austin glance in the menus while I rattle off Hannah's meal and some appetizers for the group.

"Are you ready to order or do you want her to come back after she puts in Hannah's meal and our appetizers?" I ask.

Paige looks over the edge of the menu. She's debating and Austin folds his menu, smiling up at the waitress.

"Why don't you put those in and bring us both a Corona?" He glances at Paige and gets a nod in response.

The waitress wanders off.

"My daddy says you know magic," Hannah asks, pulling Paige's attention away from the menu.

"I know a little," she says. "Why do you ask?"

"Can you create a spell to keep my castle safe?" she asks with such sincerity that an amused smile finds its way to my lips.

I trade a glance with Austin and his bemused smile says enough, and I focus elsewhere to drown out the stream of his thoughts. I don't want to eavesdrop, and sometimes I can control the stream flowing into my brain, especially in crowded places like the restaurant. I turn it all to static by not focusing on anyone in particular. At first, the din is overwhelming and I have to curb the instinct to cover my ears, but after a few deep breaths, I am able to bring it all to a low background buzz, like white noise.

The waitress steps back to our table carrying a tray of appetizers and drinks, as well as Hannah's meal.

The three of us order dinner and as soon as the waitress steps away, Paige leans over the table towards Hannah.

"Is the castle something you cherish more than anything else?"

Hannah's eyebrows arch and she glances at her work, biting her lip as she studies the sand. She slowly shakes her head, but I can tell from her melancholy expression that she is coming to terms with losing it already.

"No," she finally whispers and stares at the food on her plate.

"Then magic isn't something you want to turn to in this case. Magic, whether for good or for bad, requires sacrifice. If you aren't using it for someone you cherish, it isn't worth the price, however small it may be."

The more Paige says, the more she reminds me of my wife in her beliefs, and I turn away, scanning the rest of the patrons, letting the white noise dull the sudden ache in my chest.

"My daddy said you might be able to teach me to use magic," Hannah says, and I meet Paige's glance.

"I'd be happy to teach you the Wiccan principles," Paige smiles. "Do you know the first rule?"

Hannah glances from Paige to me, and back.

Even I know the first principle.

"Do no harm?" Hannah asks, like she isn't sure. It's something her mother would tell her from time to time.

"Yes," Paige nearly shouts, and she grins at my daughter as if she just answered the million-dollar question.

Her enthusiasm pulls a smile to my lips, and I focus on Austin while my daughter and Paige chatter about Wiccan principles.

"She's going to be a handful," he says, pointing his chin at Hannah.

"Tell me something I don't know." I can't help it. I let out a quiet laugh. "I have no idea how I'm going to pull this single dad thing off."

"Well, it certainly looks like you're pulling it off just fine."

I raise my drink, and he taps his bottle to the glass. "Thanks," I mutter, uncomfortable with compliments as a whole, but Austin has only seen a few interactions between my daughter and me, so I know he's just being kind.

I reach into my shirt pocket and drop the card he gave Bridget on the center of the table. His easy smile shifts and his shoulders tense in response. His eyes become guarded, and he can't hide his discomfort. Even if I wasn't a mind reader, all the physical cues radiating from him point to fear.

"I meant no disrespect," he says, pulling Paige's attention to ours.

I let out a little laugh. "You know, until a year ago, no one was afraid of me. Except maybe the ghosts I confronted." I keep eye contact with Austin. "I'm a third-degree black belt and no one ever batted an eye at that, but then I became supercharged and everyone becomes skittish around me, like I'm going to lash out unjustly."

"People who are unstable are unpredictable," Austin says, leaning back in his seat.

His quiet challenge starts a slow simmer inside me, but I'll be damned if I get aggravated in front of my daughter. Especially since she is now quiet and observing the tense dynamics.

"Are you mad at my daddy?" Hannah asks in a voice soft enough not to drive attention to us.

I glance down at her and she is staring at Austin with wide eyes full of surprise.

"No. I'm just worried about your father," he says, and her gaze jumps to mine.

"Austin believes in magic, but he doesn't believe in angels," I say and shrug. "He thinks I'm nuts."

Hannah looks between us and then picks at her food, unsure of what to say. The tension increases and Paige clears her throat. Hannah looks up and flips her hair over her shoulder.

"My daddy's a hero," she says with all the conviction in the world, and I huff a laugh at her sincere and stubborn set of her chin. Her glare challenges Austin to say otherwise.

Austin puts his hands up in surrender and smiles at Hannah.

"I never said he wasn't. He came to my rescue as well, so I can't argue with you there. But some things your father told me today are a little hard to believe, and it worries me."

"My daddy doesn't lie," she says, narrowing her eyes and I can't help but fill with humbleness at her defensive attitude.

"So, you grew up here?" Paige asks, trying to distract us from the tension that blankets the table.

"Yes," I answer, focusing on her, and very glad for the interruption. I really don't want to alienate the potential friendship we have. I've done enough alienating as it is today.

"It's a pretty town," she adds, and picks at the hors d'oeuvres.

"I can't imagine living anywhere else. Even though it's a summer town, busy as all get out from

Memorial Day to Labor Day, the calm of the fall and winter makes it an ideal hideaway."

"What's the hospital like?" Austin asks.

I shrug. "A hospital?" I'm not sure what he's digging for. "My experiences there haven't been horrible, despite the circumstances, but if you're looking for more details of what might be available for jobs, well, I'd refer you to Valerie. She's been working there since she finished her residency and as far as I know, she loves it."

It takes me a few seconds to catch up with his thought process.

"Are you really thinking of relocating?"

He takes a breath and then scans the ocean behind me. "I could get used to a view like this."

Paige's eyebrows rise, but it's more that of hope than surprise. "Really?"

"I'd love to see what residencies they offer," he says, and smiles over at her.

"Did you want to talk to Valerie before you leave?"

Austin gives a non-committal shrug.

Hannah is quiet and staring off at the beach. I turn in time to see the first wave hit her castle, crumbling the outer wall. I lay my hand on her back and she turns to me with a sheen of tears.

"Look at it this way. It's nature's way of giving you a new canvas to work on tomorrow," I say, and she blinks as my words sink in.

"Will you help me build a sandcastle tomorrow?"

I smile at her innocence. "Of course. It's Saturday and I don't have to go to the office until Monday. So, I'm all yours for the weekend."

"Just you and me?" she asks, hope flaring in her eyes.

"If that's what you want, you've got it."

It's amazing how much both her face and her aura light up when she is happy. I nailed it this time, and I glance up at Paige and Austin. Their auras are a little more reserved, but they both held a smile.

"York is a great place to raise kids," I say, and offer a smile. "Classes are small enough, so you get the personal attention, and the town is very much engaged in the school sports."

"Really?" Austin asks.

"Yes. At least they were when I was on the football team in high school. Everyone came out of the woodwork for home games." I glance at both

Paige and Austin. "Neither of you were into sports in high school, were you?"

Paige shakes her head. "Sorry, no. I was more of a bookworm," Paige says. "I went to an occasional game, but it really wasn't my scene."

"I was actually on the soccer team," Austin says. "It never drew the same crowd as the football games did."

"You played soccer?" Paige glances at him in surprise.

"In high school and college," he says with a grin.

The waitress stepped to our table, passing out plates to the three of us before retreating just as quickly.

"You two don't talk much, do you?" I ask, knowing it probably pushes the line, but it just pops out of my mouth and the light conversation goes dark as both their gazes lock on mine.

"We talk," Austin mutters, but there is something in his tone that tells me otherwise.

Paige glances toward the crumbling sandcastle.

"I'm sorry," I mumble. "Raven always said my candor was going to get me in trouble someday. I guess relying on sign language and people to translate sometimes buffered it."

"You say what's on your mind. That's refreshing," Paige says and digs into her meal.

I laugh. "Well, it all depends on what comes out of my mouth. I don't seem to have a handle on editing my words now that I can speak." I glance at Hannah, happy to see her eating her chicken tenders now. "I used to be a bit more diplomatic," I add, meeting her gaze again.

Austin quietly picks at the food on his plate. His gaze darts to Hannah before he sends a sideways glare in Paige's direction. The tension in his jaw makes his muscle twitch, and he turns back to the lobster stew in front of him, digging in without comment.

I'm not sure what to say, so I focus on the baked stuffed lobster on my plate.

The sound of silverware against china fills the void and before I know it, the plates are cleared, and the waitress is asking us for our dessert order.

"Can I have a sundae?" Hannah asks, her eyes as big as saucers.

I know I'll regret this later, but I nod. "Bring two spoons," I say, because I know my daughter will have two or three spoonfuls and be done.

The waitress smiles and turns towards Paige and Austin. They both order the New York Cheesecake, and the waitress moves away again.

"That was superb," Austin says.

"Try the Inn tomorrow night, and have them charge it to your room. Order the Colligan Filet, and then we can talk about a good meal."

Despite the underlying tension, they both relax with my offer, and the rest of the meal goes by without another incident. As we are walking out, Hannah pulls me towards the beach.

"I want to see the last of the castle disappear!"

I glance at Paige and Austin.

"I'd like to see it as well," Paige says. "Will you walk with me?" she asks Hannah and puts her hand out. With no hesitation, my daughter takes her hand and starts leading her down the beach towards the bathhouse.

Austin steps by my side and watches them for a moment before he turns to me.

"It's been tough," he says with a sigh. "And you were right. We don't really talk much, because every time we do, it circles around to what happened at that warehouse."

"That's a hard situation."

"Every time I go to touch her, she flinches," he admits, and I shift my stance, uncomfortable with where this conversation is going.

Raven never flinched with me, ever, so I could not relate. Her nightmares were another story, and they rivaled mine. Instead of drawing from my experiences, I inspected the catalog of CJ's memories that I had stored in my head.

"Do you love her?" I ask, and start a slow stroll in the direction Hannah and Paige went.

"Yeah," he answers, and shoves his hands in his pockets. "I should know how to navigate this shit. I've worked at the sanitarium for long enough to understand how to handle this, but it doesn't seem to work."

"Maybe you just need to talk and not handle it," I say, using finger quotes around the words 'handle it.' "She doesn't need another shrink."

Austin stops and levels that stare that I'm used to from CJ. The one that tells me I've said more than enough, and I need to shut up.

"Look. Have you dealt with what happened?" I ask, stopping and turning his way. "I only ask because it happened to both of you. She was fucked up on every level, but she seems to be handling it, from what I can tell. You're not. You're still stuck in that mental rut that you can't seem to get past."

"You don't know shit about me," he literally snarls at me.

"Do you approach her with kid gloves, or do you just let the moment happen?"

His jaw drops and he walks, passing me without comment, and I follow, letting him lead the way. The girls have taken a seat on the sidewalk at the point where the sandcastle still partially stands, and we are far enough away so our conversation cannot be heard.

Austin stops and turns. "What the fuck, man?"

I put my hands up. "Look, I'm just calling what I'm seeing. Did you even discuss what I talked to you about earlier with her, or did you just shut her down because you don't think she can handle it?"

"She wants to move here where it's safe," he says, and I now understand her reaction to his question about the hospital.

"And you shut her down." I glance over his shoulder, and Paige glances in our direction.

Austin's hands land on his hips, and he looks down at the sidewalk. "If..." He starts and trails off, shaking his head and turning toward Paige. "If we move here, I have a feeling I'd lose her."

"Why?"

"I think she has a thing for you." His hands slide into his pockets.

Laughter chokes from my throat and he glares over his shoulder. "You've got to be fucking kidding me."

Austin shakes his head. "She responds to you."

"It's because I don't treat her like damaged goods. No one wants to be treated that way. Trust me, I've been there and resented the hell out of it."

I step by his side and together we watch Paige and Hannah watching the ocean strip the castle of sand. They are smiling and laughing and Paige's aura flares bright, just like my daughter.

"We all are damaged in some way and none of us like to be reminded of it. Our nightmares are enough, so during the hours we are awake, we want to be treated like anyone else. Like nothing bad ever happened to us. With how you're treating her, it's a constant reminder of what she went through." I offer a shrug. "So basically, your training isn't doing shit right now."

"You really need to learn how to self-regulate your thoughts," Austin mutters and glances at me.

"Yeah, well, if I kept my mouth shut and did the polite thing, you two would drift farther apart, and then Hunter wins. Right?" I meet his stare. "So, drop the clinical attitude and treat her like the girl you are in love with."

# Chapter 8

ONDAY MORNING CAME TOO fast and I glance at the clock on my nightstand. It isn't even five yet and I'm wide awake, stressing over what the hell is going to happen in the office today. I don't even know if Bridget will show up for work or not, and if she's there when I get in, I have no clue of what to say.

After a half hour of staring at the ceiling, I close my eyes and send feelers out to CJ, testing whether or not he is awake.

*I'm awake. What the hell are you doing up at this hour?* His voice echoes in my head and I smile. Having a newborn throws off any sort of normal sleep pattern.

*Can't sleep.* I am hesitant to ask him to take Hannah this early, but I had agreed to let CJ and Valerie take care of her while I went to work today. It's a step in the right direction, but dropping her at their cottage at five in the morning is pushing the envelope.

*And you want to go to work instead of staring at the ceiling.*

I huff a light laugh. My brother knows me too well. "Yeah," I say aloud and transmit the thought. "Hannah is still sleeping and probably will be until around eight," I add, with a yawn.

*Do you want me to come over until she wakes up?*

I remain quiet, debating.

*Valerie doesn't mind. Alex just settled down again, so he'll be good for another couple of hours.*

"Okay. Give me fifteen minutes."

*Will do.*

I climb out of bed and hit the shower, cleaning up and dressing before the knock on the door comes. When I swing the door open, I'm glad I opted for shorts and a t-shirt. It's already uncomfortably warm, and the sun hasn't even reached the horizon.

"Mind if I crash on the couch?" CJ asks as he steps inside.

"Go ahead," I wave him inside. "I appreciate this." That itchy anxiety of leaving Hannah sets itself in the pit of my stomach and CJ pauses halfway across the room, turning back to me.

"I promise she will be fine," he says, keeping my gaze. CJ doesn't make promises he can't keep, but even that doesn't settle these false nerves.

"I know, it's just..." I trail off, knowing he is intimately familiar with the panic biting at me. It took him more than a year not to have an anxiety attack when Valerie was out of sight. I don't want to leave, but I can't keep such a tight grip on Hannah all the time, and right now, I'm finding it nearly impossible to step out the door.

"It gets easier every time," he says in response to my hesitation. "And I know I have to get off my ass and start knocking those portals off the list," he adds as he falls onto the couch.

I say nothing, instead I just give him the usual curt nod and step outside before I lose my nerve. The farther away I go, the more my stomach knots, and by the time I pull into the office driveway, I am so tense, I'm sure if someone jumps out of the bushes, my power would go all ninja on them without my permission.

I step into my office and drop my keys on my desk before heading to start a pot of coffee. I'm so wound up that the fact the light is on doesn't register until I am standing in the doorway. Any fog in my brain clears at the sight of Bridget, in a baby doll nightgown, with her back towards me. She is already filling the coffee carafe with water.

When she turns, a startled yelp fills the room and the glass pot falls from her grip. Before the pot can hit the floor and shatter into a million shards, I will it to stop.

We stare at each other in the silence. Her wide hazel eyes and her bed-ruffled hair catch me completely off guard, and that animalistic hunger is back. My eyes slowly scan her from head to toe and back.

"I, um..." I have no idea what to say, and all I do is point at the coffee pot suspended a foot from the floor.

She drops her gaze and plucks it out of the air with a mumbled thank you, but the motion gives me a peek at her chest before she straightens. She turns away and pours the water into the coffeemaker and when she does, her nightgown rides up enough for me to see the lace panties barely covering her ass.

Her aura is as chaotic as I'm sure mine is, and after she slides the pot onto the hotplate, she flips the on switch and turns in my direction.

Crossing her arms to cover herself, she stares at me.

"What are you doing here at this hour?"

I'm too stunned to speak, so I just offer a one-shouldered shrug. Unlike her, there is no easy way to hide my reaction. When her eyes fall to my tented shorts, she raises an eyebrow and meets my gaze again.

Heat fills my face, but I'm afraid to move because I have a feeling if I do, it will to be to cross the room and fuck her right there on the kitchen counter. Instead, I utter a nervous laugh.

"I guess seven weeks is a long time," I say, and it's the truth. I don't think I've gone seven weeks without sex since I was fourteen, and seeing her in that skimpy, sexy as hell outfit isn't doing anything for my self-restraint.

"Try three years," she says and lets her arms fall to her sides. She glances towards the stairway and then back at me. Her thoughts muddled between a graceful escape and doing the same thing my mind is focused on.

"I thought you didn't want to sleep with me," I say, meeting her hungry stare.

"Yeah, well, when presented with such a sexy package, I'm not exactly sure what I want." She waves at me from the other side of the room.

I blink, and then her words penetrate my brain. "Three years?" I cock my head at her.

"I haven't been with anyone since Andy died," she says and like that, her mind is made up and she bolts for the stairs, opting for escape.

I follow, because my brain isn't the one in charge right now and that high school mentality kicks in at the unspoken challenge. She hears me and before I can grab her to stop her aggravated march, she spins in my direction.

"What?" she snaps. "Isn't it enough that you scared the hell out of me in the kitchen?"

Her glare catches me off guard and I pull my hand away. The heat that drove me up the stairs fizzles. "I didn't know you'd already moved in. I'm sorry for scaring you."

"You should be. You haven't set foot in the office before nine since I started. Why are you here at five in the morning?"

"I was hoping to avoid you." The words tumble out before I can catch them.

The tiny widening of her eyes tells me I've shocked the hell out of her, and when they narrow along with her lips, I know I'm in trouble.

"You're still an asshole," she spins and marches into the bedroom at the end of the hall and slams the door. The cabinets that had been in her room line the hallway, and I focus on those instead of the blooming aggravation in my stomach. The office doors open, and I will the cabinets one by one into the meeting space. Two in each room, and as the last two are floating at my direction, she opens the bedroom door.

Keeping my concentration on the cabinets, I look at her as the furniture completes my silent instruction. She's donned a bathrobe to hide her little negligee and a layer of disappointment crumbles my concentration and the cabinets drop in place with a unified thud.

Instead of hitting this head on, I turn to go back downstairs.

"Why?"

I stop with my back to her. "Because I miss my wife, and wanting to fuck you to ease that pain is wrong." Voicing the shit turning my stomach into a knot doesn't feel any better. As a matter of fact, it makes me feel every bit the asshole she accused me of being.

# Chapter 9

I STARE OUT THE window from my desk, ignoring the chatter coming from the outer office as I have for the past two months. Ever since I ran into her in the kitchen, Bridget and I have avoided each other the best we can.

Any interaction is cordial and brief. It's like having a stranger in the outer office. And the tension between us is almost visible when we are in the same room.

I've gotten used to not having Hannah with me during the day, but I make it a point to make a daily run home to see her at lunchtime. Sometimes I ditch the rest of the day and hang out with her at the beach, or we watch the construction on the house. It's almost completed, and I am eager to get back in a home instead of a tiny rental cottage.

CJ's house is complete, and from what he said last night, they'll have the furniture moved in by the time I pick up Hannah. The timeline given to me for my home is mid-November, which means I'm hosting Thanksgiving, according to the family.

The knock on my door interrupts my thoughts and I turn my chair, meeting Bridget's gaze. She stands uncertainly in the doorway, with a piece of paper in her hand.

"What's up?"

She glances at the paper. "I think you need to look into this one," she says and crosses, handing me the note.

The seriousness in her gaze straightens my spine, and I take the information, reading her meticulous notes. "They think their house is haunted?" I raise my gaze, and she nods. I lean back in the chair, studying her. "Where's Damian?"

"He left early to go pick out furniture."

I bite the side of my lip. I rarely go on a ghost chase without a backup.

"You want to come with?"

I've seen Bridget shocked before, but this time, the visible jaw drop, and the arched eyebrows bring some humor into the awkwardness between us.

"Really?" she asks when she finds her voice.

"It might be handy having someone else who can see ghosts." I give her a shrug. "So, are you game?"

She blinks a few times, looks around my office, and then the biggest smile I've ever seen appears on her face. It glows as much as her aura.

"Hell, yeah!"

I can't help but laugh at her enthusiasm. "It isn't that glamorous," I say and stand, gathering my keys. I pause and turn towards the closet, where I stowed Raven's bag. I cross and unzip the top, rifling through the contents before I find what I am looking for. Before the shot to my stomach can take hold, I zip up her duffle bag and close the closet. It's been close to four months since she died, and this is the first time I've opened her bag. I take a second to push the pain back down before I turn back to Bridget.

"You might need this," I say, holding out the silver chain that has a Celtic Knot made of bloodstone.

Bridget stares at it and then raises her gaze. "It's beautiful," she whispers, and takes it gingerly from my hand.

"It's bloodstone," I say, and her gaze shoots to mine.

She knows what killed Raven, so she knows how hard retrieving that from her stash is. I can hear her mind working through the facts, and thankfully, she isn't reading anything into the gesture.

"It's for protection, right?"

"Yes. If there is a ghost causing problems, the likelihood of it trying to attack us is pretty high. This protects us from possession, but not anything else."

"So, an angry ghost can hurt us?" Her enthusiasm dips a notch.

"Yes." I did not want to sugarcoat this. If she is going to accompany me, she needs all the facts.

"Have you ever gotten hurt?"

I chuckle. "No. I had Damian backing me up, but now that I'm supercharged like he and CJ, I'm the backup."

"And I'm the helpless loser?" she asks and clasps the necklace around her neck.

I smile and shrug. "You said it, not me."

"Fuck you, Ryan. Let's go get us a ghost." She turns and heads out. I grab my phone off the desk and follow.

"So, we're on a last name basis?" I ask, mocking her over the roof of the car.

"It's better than me calling you asshole, don't you think?" She slides into the passenger seat, and I take a breath. I haven't said more than two words to her since I caught her in the kitchen in her negligee.

"I guess I deserve that," I say and take the driver's seat, pushing the start button while I glance at her.

"Seriously, why are you taking me on this ghost hunt?"

"Because I've been a dick long enough." I give her a strained smile and punch in the address on my GPS system. I take a second to shoot a text to Damian and CJ, telling them I'll be later than normal tonight, before I put the car in gear. "And I thought it would be refreshing to have someone with me who can tell me when something is coming at me from the opposite direction."

"You sure this isn't some elaborate plot to get rid of me?"

I utter a laugh. "Yeah, that's my plan. Just like your plan is to seduce me and steal all my money."

She actually bursts out laughing. "I'm not after your money, Tom."

I glance at her. "I know." I note she didn't deny trying to seduce me, and that familiar stirring flutters in my stomach. I follow the GPS, letting the quiet filter between us until we are a few minutes from our destination.

"When we get there, the first thing we need to do is assess the situation. If it's as dangerous as they say, we will need the owners of the house to leave."

"Okay. And then what?"

"Well, if we can start a dialog, we might not need to call in the cavalry."

"What do you mean?"

"If the ghost can listen to reason, we can show him the way to move on. Otherwise, Raven taught me a banishment spell that traps the ghost so they can't exercise their will on the physical world."

I open the console between us and pull out a small satchel, handing it to her. "Hang onto that. It has what we need for the spell."

Bridget unzips the bag and peers inside before closing it and glancing at me. "And if this doesn't work?" She holds up the bag, shaking it to prove her point.

"Then I have to call on the only person I know who can wield angel fire."

Silence captured the car, and I glance at her as we pull onto the road. Our destination is less than a quarter mile away on the right.

"How many times have you had to do that?"

I'm glad she doesn't ask who has that power, but from the clatter in her mind, she already knows my brother is the one I'm referring to.

"Twice."

"And how many ghosts hunts have you gone on?"

As I pull into the driveway, I silently count the ghost encounters Damian and I have had over the past five years. "I don't know. Over a hundred?" I say and turn off the car.

"So, your failure rate is less than two percent."

I can't help but smile. "I guess. Let's go." I don't wait for the other swarming questions to pass her lips. Instead, I step out of the car and cross to the door, with her following behind me. Before I can knock, the door swings open and I stare into the eyes of a terrified teenage girl.

"Tammy?" Bridget says from behind me.

Her eyes dart to Bridget's and she nods. "Are you from the paranormal investigation agency?"

"Yes," both Bridget and I say in unison. The clatter in the house pulls my attention from her face and I stiffen. "Maybe you should step outside," I add.

"It's hurting my mother," she whispers, and I move her onto the front step, meeting Bridget's gaze.

"Stay with her," I order, and before I step into the house, I take the satchel from her hand. She gives me a nod and her eyes transition from me to the opening of the house like it's a portal to hell. Fortunately, she has never seen a portal. This is child's play in relation to one of those abominations.

"Tom?"

I glance back at her.

"Be careful," she says and her eyes echo her plea.

I turn away from her concern and step over the threshold. The turmoil within the walls is palpable and I resist the sudden tension clenching every muscle. A shuffle behind me turns my head in that direction and I meet Bridget's wide-eyed gaze.

"Where's the girl?" I ask, suddenly annoyed with her for not following my orders.

"Locked in the car."

Her gaze darts away from me and the front door slams closed, trapping us in the house of horrors. Muffled screams come from the room down the hall, and I take a deep breath, putting my aggravation on the shelf, and focusing on the situation at hand.

"Watch my back," I say.

"Ditto," she answers. When she pulls out a mini gun from her pocketbook, I raise my eyebrows.

"Put that thing away before you shoot someone." The admonishment in my tone is clear, and her frazzled gaze meets mine.

She presses her lips together and flips the safety back on before she stows it away at my request.

"Bullets don't hurt ghosts, but they can kill both of us," I say, and focus down the hall again. I understand her rationale. It's for her own sense of control, but a gun in the realm of the paranormal is not a smart move. Angry ghosts can and will use whatever weapon they can get their hands on. Getting bloody doesn't bother me, but I'm not ready to die just yet. I keep that tidbit to myself and proceed with caution.

I step into the entry to the family room and halt. The scene is right out of a violent movie or an x-rated porn flick. I can't decide which and the sheer number of ghosts partaking shocks me to inaction. Their auras are as black as the thick Maine woods on a moonless night.

Tammy's mother's arms are bound at the wrist and she hangs from the ceiling while the pack of ghosts accost her. Bruises line the skin that is visible through her shredded clothing, and I now understand why her screams are muffled and why Tammy was so fucking freaked out.

A silent admonishment recoils through me. I should have done some research on the address before coming here, then maybe I'd know what the hell to do. I'm actually at a loss.

"What the hell?" Bridget announced our presence, and the pack turns in our direction, stopping their assault on the homeowner. She crumples to the ground, sobbing, as their collective focus looks right through me.

The air actually makes a popping sound when they disappear, and I shiver with the shock of it. I'm not sure what the fuck we are dealing with at all, and I scan the room in front of me. It isn't until I hear a yelp and a thud behind me that my heart jumps in my throat. I spin and Bridget is pinned to the wall with a ghostly hand covering her mouth. Rope wraps around her wrists, pulling her arms overhead in the same position as the homeowner. I shiver as their filthy hands start their exploration amidst her muffled scream for help. Her wide, terrified eyes mirror that of the woman sobbing behind me.

Reality slams home. If I don't do something now, they are going to hurt her in ways she will never fully recover from. A protective wave surges through me, wrapped in anger.

"Leave her alone!" The voice bellows from my chest in an inhuman growl. The power in me blurs my vision, and heat encompasses every cell. When her shirt rips and the button on her jeans unlatch, I can't control the fury. It lashes out and the horde of ghosts is thrown in every direction. Bridget slides to the ground, her breathing raspy, and her eyes wide with fear.

I unzip the satchel and dump the contents on the ground, uttering the Latin words that comprise Raven's banishing spell. My voice is unsteady with the adrenaline and doubt rushing my system. Usually Damian reads the words, so I'm praying I have the right accent, otherwise I might just be brewing things to a different level.

The explosion of the spell knocks me on my ass and the ghostly screams of protest fill the small house. Bridget covers her ears, but my erratic heartbeat muffles the sound. I stare at the writhing mass above me as they fight against the chains I've locked them in.

Murderous promises hurl through the space between us, and I'm not sure the spell will keep. I don't want to end up being a ghost's bitch, and I can't watch them hurt Bridget.

It's time to call the cavalry before they get loose.

My thought barrels from my core loud enough to wake CJ, or at least make him bolt out of whatever seat he's parked in. A phone call in this situation isn't enough and I'm sure the panic filling me came through loud and clear.

The air ripples next to me and CJ appears. I project what I'm seeing right into his head and with a cool inhale of breath; he closes his eyes. Angel fire builds in his aura, making me squint, but I can't look away as it forms wings on his back before it fully encompasses him. When his eyelids fly open, the white fire shoots like a bolt of lightning, engulfing the raging ghosts.

It's over in seconds and CJ glances at me, and that cocky smile I want to punch appears just before he pops out of existence. I'm sure I'll hear more about how stupid I was to bring Bridget into this when I get home, but for now, I turn my attention to the conditions around me.

The quiet is deafening, and I sit on the floor, getting my bearings before I lock my gaze with Bridget. This is so much more disturbing than any of the past ghost hunts I have encountered, and I have a second to wonder if what happened earlier this summer opened up some door between our world and the next.

# Chapter 10

AFTER GETTING TAMMY'S MOTHER to the emergency room, I drive back to the office with Bridget in the passenger seat. Neither of us speaks, and I go directly to the kitchen pantry, pulling out a bottle of whiskey, pouring two shots before I stow the bottle. I turn and offer Bridget one.

She takes it and we tap the glasses together before downing the shot. I lean against the counter with my eyes closed, letting the burn flow down my throat, the scrape of a chair opens my eyes. Bridget sits at the table with her face in her hands.

"I shouldn't have brought you," I whisper, and she turns her head towards me. The dampness on her cheeks glistens in the light, and I sigh.

"Did you know you have black wings?"

"Excuse me?" I can feel the arch of my eyebrows.

"Right before you knocked the ghosts away from me, I swear I saw black wings spread from your back. Like you're some kind of fallen angel, or something."

I laugh and run my hand through my hair. The only angel I ever saw with black wings was Lucifer, and the thought chills me.

"You really weren't kidding about being angel blood." She leans back in her seat studying me.

"No. I wasn't." I glance away, because her words are still pinging around my head. Black wings. CJ has the heavenly white wings and mine reflects the devil. Well, shit. That just ruins my night, and I turn away, staring out the window.

Her hand lands on my shoulder and I try to shrug it off, but she steps to my side, reaching out and turning my face in her direction.

"You saved that woman today. And you saved me. Thank you."

I can't help but laugh. "CJ saved everyone, like he always does," I say, and direct my gaze away from her, but I don't pull away from her lingering touch.

When her thumb caresses my bottom lip, my eyes turn back to hers.

"I haven't felt that... alive in a very long time," she says, with her gaze focused on my lips. She licks her own and her eyes dart to mine. Hunger lives there.

"I'm one of Lucifer's descendants." The words wrap in bitterness, but she doesn't shy away.

"And Raphael's if that list is correct," she says, making me feel like less of a freak. When she leans in, I let her.

The gentle press of her lips against mine opens a door I had closed tight two months ago. Logic goes by the wayside, and I wrap my arms around her, pulling her tighter against me. There is no fight this time, and when her lips part, allowing my tongue access, I'm overwhelmed with the sensation. The movement of our tongue dance captivates me, and I pull her closer, breathing in the fresh scent of her.

"Tommy, stop," she whispers under my lips and her hands push on my chest.

I take a step back and put my hands out with my palms facing her. We remain in place and I'm not sure if it is aggravation or want making my heart pulse in my ears. We are inches away from each other, and her ragged breath matches mine. I search her eyes as her aura pulses, giving away the want she is feeling just as acutely as I am.

"I haven't been with anyone for so long..." she whispers and reaches out, placing her palm on my chest. It isn't to push me away, it's to feel my heartbeat, and she stares at the contact.

"Maybe I should go," I say and utter a sigh.

Bridget turns her gaze outside, giving the slightest of nods before looking back at me. "What if I don't want you to?" She bites her lower lip now that the thoughts swarming in her mind have trickled out.

She has the good sense to take a step back, distancing herself from me. "This probably isn't a good idea," she says, but the juxtaposition of her words and her actions as she licks her lips just adds fuel to my already stoked fire.

"Why not?" I advance a step closer, letting my carnal desires out of the locked cabinet in my soul.

I need the human connection. I need to let this tension between us ignite.

"Because you are not ready for this," she says, and her voice has that breathy quality that I remember from our encounter back in high school.

Memories flood my brain and I'm not sure if they are hers or mine or a potent concoction of both, but the effect has me stalking her, trying to maneuver her towards the stairwell and her bedroom on the second floor. This does not go unnoticed by that little voice in my head, but my mind is decidedly not in control at the moment.

"But you are," I whisper and close the distance, leaning in and delivering another heat filled kiss. The sensations drown out any warning my brain tries to launch. When her hands pull at the hem of my shirt, I peel it off, pulling away from her mouth for just a split second. Which gives me just enough time to see the iridescent pink of raw lust painted in her aura.

I lick a line from her clavicle to her ear, and she shivers, letting out a squeal. Her skin tastes like sweat and honey and as I nibble on her earlobe and attempt to undress her, I wonder what her pussy will taste like. I can't seem to work the buttons on her shirt and with a growl, I rip it apart, sending buttons bouncing across the kitchen tile.

"Tommy," she says in a gasp as I pick her up and set her on the kitchen counter. She wraps her legs around me, pulling me closer as our lips connect again.

The madness of this moment engulfs me and I home in on every sensation, from her tongue twirling with mine, to the hardness of her nipples under the thin fabric of her bra.

"I want to taste every fucking inch of you," I whisper, breaking the kiss. She moans when my mouth trails down to her chest. I tease her with my tongue, tracing the edge of her bra while I reach around her back and flick the clasp, freeing her from the fabric.

Bridget's breasts are beautiful, and I stare at them, rubbing her nipples with my thumbs, and meeting her gaze. The grin slowly stretches my lips and I lean in, but this time I avoid her lips and catch the underside of her jaw, trailing kisses until I have her hard nipple in my mouth.

I explore every inch of her breasts with my tongue and my hands run up her jean-clad thighs. Her hands are buried in my thick hair, and her soft purrs when I do something she likes guides me along with the hints freely accessible in her mind.

Her thoughts toggle between the pure heat and wanting to stop before we step into the land of regret, but she voices neither. Instead, her thoughts tangle in the sensation, just the way mine do.

She leans back on the counter, allowing me access to the buttons on her jeans. I explore her belly button with my tongue while tugging at the fabric. There is no easy way to take her jeans off without destroying the current mood we are both in, so I do something I've only seen in a memory. I will the fabric to shred.

Bridget gasps, and her grip on my hair tightens. I send a playful glance up at her, and then nip at her inner thigh. She sucks in her breath when I pass over her clit with only a cursory flick of my tongue. I'm too far gone to care about the ramifications of my actions. I want to taste her. I want to feel her come. I want to hear her moan my fucking name.

When I take a knee and cover her clit with my mouth, she lifts her leg onto the counter, leaning on one hand while the other has a solid grip on my hair. I roll my tongue around the nub, and she groans.

Her reaction burns just as hot as the fire raging inside me. With her hands still webbed in my hair, she moans, widening her legs, begging me with her thoughts until her mouth echoes the same sentiments.

"Oh, fuck," she whispers, and her body shudders with her first release.

Tasting her hot nectar drives me further over the edge and the salty sweetness fuels my need. I continue to drive her over the edge until she's dripping on the counter and her juices coat my lips and my fingers.

My cock is so hard I'm not sure I can get my jeans over my hips, but I manage, and in one motion, I stand and bury my cock inside her before she can catch her breath.

"Oh, my god," she whispers and wraps her legs around my waist.

Every hip thrust is met with the same bravado, and Bridget arches into me, pulling me to her lips again. I plunge my tongue into the recess of her mouth, exploring, tasting, enjoying every sensation accosting my body.

The heat pulls from my fingers and toes, pooling in my belly until it's burning for release. My body stiffens with the rocket of an orgasm, pulling a groan from my lips. The aftermath saps the strength out of me, leaving my muscles quivering, and I lean on the counter with my head resting on her shoulder, but I don't move yet. Not with my heart slamming against the walls of my chest like I just ran the thousand-yard dash.

"Holy shit."

Her breath tickles my ear, and my eyes focus on the cabinets behind her. Now that the physical sensations have abated, the reality of what I have just done seeps in, and I close my eyes.

Regret is a fucked-up thing, and it now has a tighter grip on me than Bridget. I know damned well I shouldn't have done this, and I really have no rightful excuse beyond just being a sex hound.

I push myself away from her shoulder and look at the woman I've just compromised, feeling like an absolute shit heel.

She blinks up at me and her easy smile fades. Her eyes dart to where we are still joined and they widen, meeting mine again.

"You didn't use anything."

My heart literally skips, and I think my jaw drops open. I know my eyes widen, and I pull out of her like she was a leper. "Fuck," I mutter, and pull my underwear and jeans up from around my ankles. It's been years since a condom entered my mind, never mind how long it's been since I had cause to use one.

"You're not..." I wave at her like she is supposed to finish the sentence, but my mind is so fuzzy with the ramifications that I can't even concentrate to hear her thoughts.

"I'm not what?" she says, and hops off the counter. She has no clothing left to put on, so she grabs my shirt from over the back of the chair where it had been tossed. "Diseased?" she asks after the fabric covers her.

"No. On the pill?" I ask, hoping for some way to not have another mistake in my life.

"No. I'm not on the pill," she says. "And it's a really shitty time to be this stupid," she adds before she disappears into the bathroom.

I'm not sure if the comment was aimed at me or not, and I just stand there like an incompetent fool waiting for instruction.

I lean against the counter we've just desecrated and stare at the floor.

"I'm sorry," I say when she steps back in the kitchen. "I never intended..." I trail off because I'm not sure if that's really the truth or not. The thing between us was not easy, like it had been with my wife. This was filled with fits and starts, battles of wills, and tension so palpable I thought I'd scream at times.

The intensity of it worried me, and I met her tentative stare.

"I didn't intend on this either. Otherwise, I would have been prepared," she adds with a little laugh.

My lips tilt in a half smile. "I guess ghost hunting sharpens the appetite."

Her light laugh answers my attempt at humor. "I thought you were good in bed back in high school, but damn, you've jumped into a whole new category all your own," she says and her cheeks fill with red blush.

"And what category would that be?" I ask, trying not to grin at the compliment.

"Beyond earth shattering," she answers, and takes a deep breath, trying to control the creep of blush that now has taken over her entire face. She shifts and utters another laugh, but this time, it's laced with nerves. "As much as I'm going to hate myself for allowing this to happen, I have to admit, it was worth every moment of awkward silence that will precede this."

"Awkward silence?" I straighten.

"Yes. Tomorrow, you're going to be all weird when you come in, like you don't know what to say to me. It will be frustrating and endearing all at once." She heads towards the stairwell and pauses, pointing at the shredded fabric all over the kitchen. "You are cleaning that up."

I huff a laugh and she challenges me with a raised eyebrow.

"Fine," I say, and she disappears up the stairs. Glancing around, I made a hell of a mess. "I'll buy you another pair of jeans," I yell up at the ceiling, hoping she can hear me.

"Damned straight you will!"

The answer pulls a smile and I grab the garbage pail from under the sink. Cleaning up is the easy part and I concentrate, willing every stitch of torn fabric into the receptacle before returning it to its place.

I rinse my face and hands in the sink and dry my face with paper towels before grabbing a couple of counter cleaning wipes. I scrub down the area we just christened, and my thoughts swirl between her comment about black wings and the way she tasted. The two thoughts didn't belong in the same zip code, never mind side by side, volleying for my attention.

She cleared her throat, making me jerk in surprise.

Her low chuckle told me she caught my startled jump, and I glance in her direction after throwing the nearly torn wipes in the garbage. Bridget tosses me my shirt and I slip it on. She's right. Now that the euphoria of the moment has faded, I'm not sure what to say.

"See. Awkward silence," she says with a sigh.

"Sorry." I shuffle my feet and glance at the clock. It's close to seven and I need to get home to my daughter. When I turn back to Bridget, she just smiles.

"Go. You've kept Hannah long enough," she says.

The sudden need to kiss her moves my feet in her direction, but she holds up her hand, stopping me.

"This was a onetime deal," she says, nodding toward the counter. "We both needed to blow off some steam, okay?"

It's more like a line I would have used to gloss over a good fuck back in high school, and it makes me more uncomfortable than I care to admit. "Sure," I say. "I'll catch you tomorrow," I add, and head out to my car without a glance over my shoulder.

In the confines of the car, I stare at the house, watching as the front lights turn off and then the kitchen, before she walks by her bedroom window a few minutes later. She pauses and pulls the curtain back. Our eyes meet across the distance.

My hand sits idle on the gears, and I take a deep breath, blowing air out in a slow stream before I put the car in reverse. One last glance and she's still standing there, watching me drive away, with her face framed in a thoughtful expression.

# Chapter 11

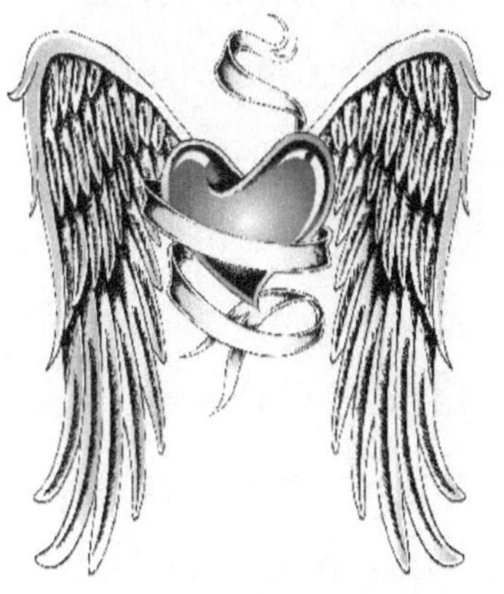

I PULL INTO CJ's house, scanning the familiar architecture. He had the builders recreate the home we grew up in, instead of making it his own. A furniture van was in the driveway, and I parked to the side. Scooting around the truck, I cross to the front door and let myself in.

Even the layout is the same, and I step into the formal living room, complete with CJ's new baby grand piano stationed in the same spot as before. The decor is minimalist, which is a bit of a divergence from our parent's warm, cluttered environment. When I step into the kitchen, all familiarity with the house ends. The kitchen and family room is much more customized, and more of a natural fit to what I envisioned as my brother's tastes. The kitchen includes an extended counter that wraps around to form a breakfast bar, as well as a sizeable island in the center of the kitchen, which is also adorned with bar stools.

They are missing a formal dining table like we had before, but the amount of sparkling granite makes up for the lack of seating. I have to admit, I'm a little impressed with the modifications.

The television is in the same place it once was. However, it's probably the biggest one CJ could find, now that the built-in cabinets are no longer gracing the wall. Despite the overbearing size of the television, the room looks bigger without the built-ins. The very comfortable looking sectional couch seems dwarfed by the room size, and I glance towards the front of the house.

They put a new kitchen table by the windows, turning the front half of the room into the dining space. I still haven't run into anyone, and I only have one room left. The exercise room—beyond the family room. I cross by new extra wide French doors leading to the backyard, glancing at the covered pool before focusing on the door to where the exercise room used to be.

I open it and stare. The room is split in two, with a glass panel separating the far room from this one. A control panel is laid out before me, and my eyes do not know where to focus, so I step into the room, inspecting the space beyond the glass. Another piano is parked there, along with microphones and egg crate foam walls. I let out a little laugh.

CJ built himself a state-of-the-art recording studio.

This is all well and good, but where the hell is my daughter?

I spin on my heels, closing the door.

"CJ?" I call out with only my voice. When no response comes, I close my eyes and reach out with my mind. They are in the house, but not where I expect. I turn and cross the kitchen, stepping beyond the first-floor powder room and into the entry to the basement. In the old house, this space was unfinished, but I glance down a fully finished stairwell with colorful berber carpeting.

I descend, and it isn't until I reach the bottom that the noise reaches my ears. The soundproofing in this place is out of this world.

"Daddy!" Hannah's excited screech pulls my attention away from the construction and into the heart of the multi-purpose room. Various exercise equipment lines the outer wall, and in the center is the biggest indoor playscape I have had the pleasure of seeing, and another large television set is being hung on the wall by the furniture company.

CJ pokes his head out from the other side of the playscape and smiles at me just as my daughter flings herself into my arms. I cross the distance and suppress a laugh at the instruction booklet laid out on the floor, along with various pieces and parts yet to be put together.

Grace and her brothers are running around through a mini-maze of toys while Valerie nurses Alex in a comfortable-looking glider.

"The house looks great," I say and put Hannah back down so she can resume playing.

"Thanks." CJ glances at the instructions and tightens a bolt before he meets my gaze. "I've been putting this monstrosity together all day." He points his screwdriver at the playscape. "The only break

I've had was when I saved your ass," he says, lowering his voice as he stares me down from his seat on the floor. "What the hell were you thinking taking her there?"

"She can see ghosts. I thought she'd be useful, but honestly, I have never seen anything like that."

He let out a laugh. "Yes, you have," he says, and I know damned well he's referring to our interception of the ghosts attacking Paige in New York.

I glance around the room again, but CJ's sharp stare pulls my gaze back to him.

"Thanks for helping me out with Hannah," I say, leaving off thanks for, yet again, saving me from myself. He's made a lifetime habit of that and right now, it irks the hell out of me.

He's still staring at me, and now his dimples appear. I realize he's trying not to smile and I form a glare. He's in my head, snooping, and now that I realize it, I can feel the alien presence.

"Really?" I say and the smile forms on his face.

"I'm the one who should be asking that," he says with a laugh.

*Fuck you.* I hurl the thought and he winces at the volume in his head. And he has the audacity to raise an eyebrow.

"I believe you've already done that today."

"What?" Valerie's voice yanks my attention in her direction. Unjust betrayal radiates from her, and I bite my lip as the guilt builds inside me.

"Leave the boy alone," CJ says, sending what I call the 'shut up' look.

"It's only been three months," she balks.

I shift my weight and shove my hands into my pockets. I feel like I'm being reprimanded by my mother, and I slide a sideways glance at Valerie. The verbal conversation is scarce enough that the kids don't pick up on it, but her sharp admonishment in my mind leaves me quiet. I'm damned if I am going to apologize to her for my behavior. If anyone needs an apology, it is Bridget.

"Hannah, it's time to pack up," I announce at the same time the technician announces his task is complete.

CJ climbs up from the floor and walks the workman out of the house. I follow him upstairs because I can't stand the judgment radiating from Valerie.

As soon as the front door closes, he turns to me with a grin. "You shut down those thoughts pretty damned quickly after my comment."

"It's none of your fucking business," I snap, glaring at him. "And I really don't need Valerie judging me right now. Opportunity presented itself and I took it."

He chuckled. "Once a whore, always a whore."

He's not talking about Bridget, and I'm not sure whether or not to punch him. My palms ache and I realize I've clenched my fists. I loosen my hands and stare at my brother.

"Yeah, well, at least I didn't let some random chick tie me up and show me what her strap on is used for."

CJ bursts out laughing. "Yeah. Okay. You've got me there." When he winds down, he sighs. "Still, are you sure she has your best interests at heart?"

I narrow my eyes. "What do you have against Bridget?"

CJ shifts and slides his hands in his pockets. "I don't know. I just have a feeling she has an ulterior motive for... everything."

This is one situation where I have more information than my brother, and I crack a smile.

"O'Keefe asked her to look after me. I guess he figured both Raven and Hannah were going to die, and he knew Bridget lived through something similar."

CJ's brow creased.

Usually CJ was quick to get the gist, but I guess sleep deprivation is taking its toll, because after a moment, I say, "Bridget can see ghosts and her uncle paid her a visit after he died."

CJ's eyes widen in understanding. "Oh." His exhausted mind mulls things over before he blinks and refocuses on me. "On a different note, Valerie is going back to work tomorrow."

It is my turn to be slow on the uptake, but after a moment, what he is trying to say seeps in. "I need to make alternate arrangements for Hannah," I say, and he nods.

"At least for a couple of weeks, while I get used to taking care of Alex on my own."

"No problem," I say, and Hannah comes running around the corner, her eyes a little wild like she thought I left without her. "Hey, peanut. You feel like coming to work with me in the morning?"

She beams and I have my answer. I glance at CJ again. "Thanks for helping for as long as you have."

"Give me a few weeks, and by that time, I'll probably be good to juggle a little more again." He glances at Hannah and messes up her hair before meeting my gaze.

"It might be time for me to find a more permanent solution." I'm almost as surprised by my words as CJ is, and I utter a soft laugh and a shrug. "Besides, I have to think about pre-school."

"Pre-school. I can't believe she's getting that old." He glances at my daughter and sighs.

"We're getting old," I say. Thirty is right around the corner for both of us, and the fact we are both still breathing blows me away, especially with all the shit we've lived through.

He scoffs at me. "Speak for yourself." He opens the front door, signaling the end of the conversation.

I scoop Hannah up in my arms and head out while she chatters endlessly about all the adventures she had today. By the time we reach the cottage, her continuous chatter is now the background noise to the memory of my own adventure.

# Chapter 12

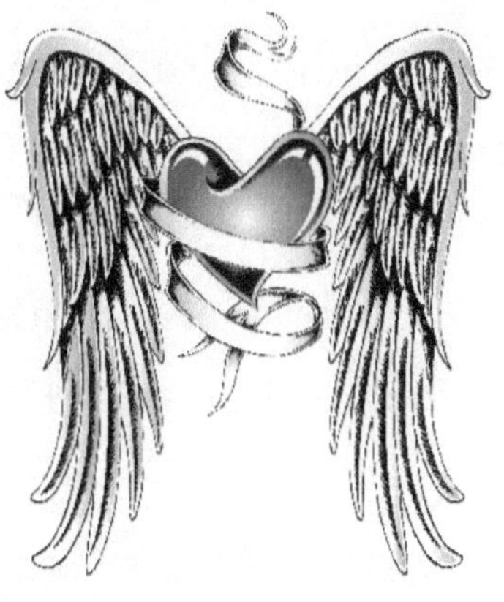

THE NEXT MORNING, I linger at the cottage, cleaning up the dishes from last night and letting Hannah wake on her own. Sleep had been restless, and now I am trying to wake from the morning stupor, and coffee isn't doing it for me.

Nightmares hit with hurricane force last night. In each one, some horrifying end came to Hannah, no matter how much I begged and pleaded. Variations put Bridget under the knife, and the resulting panic attack almost made me call her, but

I had a feeling she would roast me alive if I called her at three in the morning.

The rest of the night, I rolled from side to side and finally dragged my ass into the shower at a little past five. I've been watching the morning news for a couple of hours now and restlessness has set in. I climb to my feet and head to Hannah's room to get her moving.

The door squeaks when I swing it open, and it takes me a second to digest what I'm seeing. An empty bed meets my stare, and my gut clenches like I've just been hit with a wrecking ball.

"Hannah," I yell, spinning towards the bathroom and then my bedroom. I scour every inch of the cottage before I dart outside and bellow her name. No response and fear as hot as a stove burner on high fills every fiber of my being.

I did not hear anything. I did not wake up.

I freeze in place, unsure of what to do. I don't know how long she has been gone. She was there at midnight when I got up to make sure she was okay. The panic accosting me makes it hard to think clearly, but I had enough sense to dial nine-one-one.

"York Beach Nine-one-one, what is the location of your emergency?"

"Chapman's Cottages, Unit four," I respond. "My daughter is missing. She's three, and she was in bed when I checked on her at midnight, but she is not in the cottage." My words tumble out as my chest constricts, tightening with every second. "Oh, Jesus," I whisper as my breathing becomes ragged.

"Can I have your name, sir?" she asks, still keeping that calm voice that does nothing to stop my hyperventilating.

"Tom. Tom Ryan," I say between breaths.

"Sir, I need you to sit and put your head between your legs."

Sitting wasn't going to happen. "My daughter's gone!" I yell breathlessly. "I can't sit down, not..." I stop speaking as my better sense kicks in. Babbling about Lucifer would get me checked into the psych ward, and I didn't have time for that.

"I understand that, sir, and a cruiser already is on the way, but it sounds like you are hyperventilating and if you don't sit down and do as I ask, you will pass out," she says with that calming cadence.

She has no clue just how terrified I am, and there is no way to explain that my little girl may already be dead. The thought is like a slap, and I blink as my breath finds the right rhythm again. I, of all people, would know if she were dead.

Frigid fear slowly wraps around my heart. If she isn't dead, what the hell is the game?

"That's it, sir," the dispatcher on the phone says, and I take another slow breath.

A police cruiser pulls into the lot with its lights on but the sirens off and stops in front of my cottage. A single officer climbs out and I balk at the lack of response.

"Only one officer?" I say into the phone. "My three-year-old is missing, and God knows where, and you send only one officer?"

I can't help the growl in my voice. Didn't this nitwit know anything? I disconnect the call and stare at the approaching cop. The familiar gait raises an eyebrow.

Bear Whipple, an ex-friend from high school, approaches, and he tips his hat back when he stops in front of me. I hadn't taken notice of him at O'Keefe's funeral, but then again, I hadn't been looking for any familiar faces.

"Tom," he says with a cautious nod.

"Bear," I respond, and if I wasn't so damned panicked about Hannah, his reaction would have cracked me up. He actually steps back and points, like he just witnessed a miracle. "The last gift Raven gave to me," I say and inhale. "My daughter is missing," I add, and turn towards the cottage behind me. "I checked on her before I went to bed, but she wasn't in her room when I went to wake her."

"What time did you last see her," he asks, and crosses to look at the door.

"Around midnight." My voice cracks and Bear turns his attention to me.

"She'll be all right," he says.

I let out a high-pitched laugh. "Just like my wife would be all right?"

Bear stands from his crouch, and I catch the pity in his eyes and the remorse at screwing up our friendship back in high school.

"Look, we'll find her," he says, and I know he means well, but he has no idea what I am up against. "In the meantime, I need to radio this in. It looks like your lock was tampered with and with any luck, maybe we will get a set of prints we can work with."

Last night was the first night that all three of us were not staying here. The timing really unnerves me, and I take a seat in the small living room, feeling as if I can barely draw a breath.

After Bear comes back into the cottage, and he does a sweep of each room, he comes back and clears his throat. "I need to ask. Do you have any enemies?"

A stress laugh escapes, and I glance at him. "Not since high school," I say, knowing it's a low blow, but I can't help it. He glances down at his notepad. The red hue rises in his cheeks. "Our names were on that list that was found at the groomer's in July," I add after a moment.

When his gaze finds mine, he grimaces. "I know," he says. "The chief had us on watch for a couple of months after your wife's death, just to make sure there wasn't another attempt on your family." He glances at the ground as his mind struggles to find the words to convey his sorrow for the loss of my wife. He looks up without voicing anything running through his head.

He takes a few blinks before his professional demeanor is back. "Just on the off chance the marks on the door aren't what I think they are. Is there any way she could have wandered off while you were in the shower?" he asks.

"I don't think she would. Besides, where the hell would she go?"

It takes a second and then my gaze jumps to the road and the beach beyond.

I am moving before my brain registers and Bear is scrambling to catch up. When I get to the sidewalk bordering the beach, my heart thunders and I scan the sand, praying she came to see if her sandcastle made it through the night. She isn't on the beach and my gaze darts to the retreating surf. While I know on some level, this is all futile, and my daughter is not anywhere near York at this moment, I cling to hope that my underlying intuition is dead wrong.

"We, uh, we made a sandcastle yesterday," I say, because it is all I can croak out of my tight throat. "But she'd never cross the road by herself," I add after I swallow. I had yelled at her not to go near the road alone enough times over the summer. If she was a teenager, I wouldn't put it past her to disregard whatever I say, but at three, she listens intently and follows orders where crossing the road without an adult is concerned.

My hand runs through my hair and my stomach clenches enough that I think I might vomit my morning coffee all over the sidewalk. "Jesus," I whisper, and spin around, looking back at the cluster of cottages.

Bear's hand lands on my shoulder and I stare at it before meeting his gaze. He glances at where we were staying as well. "We'll find her," he says, but his brain is already radiating the loss.

My pocket vibrates, and I pull out my phone. The office number blinks and I connect the call.

"Damian?" I ask without waiting for salutations to be passed.

"No. It's Bridget," she says, and her voice is full of hesitation. "Are you okay?" she asks after a pause.

"Hannah's missing."

The squeak of a chair sounds in the background. "I think you need to come to the office now."

I'm already crossing the street, heading towards the cottage where my car keys are. A couple of other cruisers are now in the parking lot and police are congregated outside the cottage door.

"Why?"

"A package came with a note."

"Did you open it?"

"No. It says for your eyes only, but it also says it is urgent you open right away. First thing this morning."

I slow to a stop before I enter the cottage and trade a glance with Bear. "Don't open it. Not until I get there with the police, okay?"

"Okay, and Tom?"

"Yeah?"

"Hannah's okay."

Her conviction is sweet, but she is wrong. Hannah is in Lucifer's hands, and nothing is okay about that. I end the call and nod towards his cruiser.

"A package was delivered to my office this morning. Think you can drive me there and possibly bring the bomb squad?" I ask Bear, and refrain from requesting the animal control officer as well. The last killer used snakes to poison his victims, and I could just envision a box of writhing cobras waiting to strike.

Bear's face pales, but to his credit, he nods and speaks into the microphone clipped to his shoulder. I rattle off the address to my office and he transmits the information before pointing to the passenger side of the car.

I slide into the seat, feeling a sense of déjà vu as we take off, this time with lights and sirens. When we pull into the driveway, Bridget steps out of the front door. Her face hardens when Bear steps out of the car with me.

She doesn't approach, instead she just crosses her arms and turns back into the house.

"Bridget O'Keefe works for you?" Bear asks as we are walking toward the house.

"Yes," I answer. I don't feel like explaining myself to Bear Whipple. He follows me, but waits on the front porch for the bomb squad.

I step inside and approach the desk. "Where's the package?" I ask, glancing around, looking for a box of some sort.

She picks up a small mail pouch and hands it to me.

"This is what you pulled me here for?" I ask, holding it out as the irritation burns through the terror that had gripped me since I opened Hannah's door.

"The delivery person stressed you had to open it before nine."

We both look at the clock. I have five minutes to open the envelope. Thoughts of anthrax or something equally deadly spin in my mind, but just by the feel, I highly doubt that is what this thing contains.

"You should step outside just in case," I say, looking back at her. "And you can tell Bear it isn't a bomb."

As soon as she is out the door, I tear open the package and dump the contents into my hand. A zip drive lands in my palm and I close my eyes for a second before sitting down at the desk and plugging the drive into Bridget's already booted machine. Just for good measure, I plug in her earphones so there is zero chance of either Bridget or Bear overhearing what is on the zip drive. The only other thing in the envelope is a small piece of paper with what looks like a time stamped on it.

The minute I click on the eternal drive icon, the screen goes black. I glance at the packaging again, looking for some sign of where it originated, but there are no postmarks, or anything beyond block letters spelling my name. There isn't even an address, which I find odd, but the screen flashes and a video comes up.

All logical thought ceases as I stare at my daughter's terrified face. I have to force myself to look at her surroundings, and my stomach drops. She's in a private airplane.

His low chuckle comes over the microphone, and then the likeness of Lucifer steps into view, and I recoil. He crosses and peels her arm from her body, holding it out so I can see it.

"She is delicious," he whispers and Hannah screams as he bites her arm, drawing blood. He only drinks from her arm for a second, but when he pulls his mouth from her tender skin, he grins, showing off his blood-streaked lips and teeth. Hannah pulls her arm back to her chest. Her sobs continue.

I want to tear through the screen and destroy that bastard.

"Here's the deal," he says, pulling the camera to focus on his face. "I will trade your little bundle of joy for Damian Andreas. Bring him to Athens, Greece, by nightfall. If you deliver him to me, I will deliver your daughter to you. If you fail, I'll send you a video of what I do to her, as payment for your failure." He pauses and smiles. "If he finds out about this deal before we are face to face, I will make sure she suffers for a very long time before I kill her."

The screen goes blank.

I just stare.

"Tom?" Bridget's voice cuts though my shock and I look up from the display in front of me, yanking the drive from the side of the computer and palming it.

"Yeah?" I answer.

"Is that related to Hannah's disappearance?" she asks and I shake my head.

"No. It's a job request. Damian and I are requested in Greece." I'm not sure if I'm convincing at all, but the knot in my stomach tightens.

"I can go with him. You stay here and look for Hannah."

My gaze darts from her to Bear and back. I don't know how to pull this off. I close my mouth for a moment and turn my gaze to Bear. "There's nothing here." I push the thought. "Go back to the cottage." I add with an extra push, just for good measure.

Bear blinks and turns, wandering away. The minute the car starts and pulls out, I turn to Bridget. She stands with her arms crossed.

"I have to go to Greece with Damian."

She cocks her head at me, searching my eyes with hers. "Hannah is being taken there," she says, and it isn't a question.

My brain is flying through excuses, but I just nod. "They asked for a ransom." It's the only logical thought I can produce, and it might just be one that I can convince Damian of. "And if I don't deliver it in person, they'll sell Hannah into slavery."

"You need the police," she says, and I raise my eyebrow, challenging her.

"I need Damian to come with me on this, and I need CJ hanging tight, watching over the rest of the family."

"It's not..." she trailed off.

"No. It's a goddamned kidnapper, looking to make a buck off the filthy rich," I snap. "Call Damian and tell him to meet me at Pease airfield in an hour." I don't know if I can get Ted Beaumont at this short notice, but if I go with this story, it might light a fire under everyone's ass.

I also have to lock down my thoughts, otherwise Damian will know. And I need to come up with some sort of plan. Damian stole Lucifer's grace. If Lucifer gets it back, there is little either CJ or I can do to stop him from starting Armageddon.

# Chapter 13

I STAND AT THE terminal, waiting for the private jet Ted promised us. I'm still planning the story in my head when Damian walks in. The duffel bag at my feet contains reams of paper cut into dollar size strips, and a couple of thousand dollars spread over the paper so it actually looks like a bag of ransom money, if someone isn't taking a close inspection of the contents. I also have my nine-millimeter in a holster under my jacket. I know it's useless against the devil, but it might help with my bogus story.

Damian steps to my side. "So, what's the plan?" he asks.

I huff a laugh. "I really have no plan. We just go in and storm the castle. I think we can handle whatever they throw at us, and get Hannah out before they have a chance to hurt her."

"Do you know where in Greece we are going?"

I shake my head. "The next contact will be on the plane." I layer the bullshit some more. I really don't know when Lucifer will contact me again, but I'm willing to bet it will be when we are in the air.

"Did you get proof of life?" Damian asks.

I'm glad I had the forethought to send a picture to my phone from the video. I saved a still of Hannah that included the date and time, and showed the interior of a private plane. Nothing else was in the video except her terrified face looking directly into the lens.

Damian whistled through his teeth. "And you're sure it isn't our mutual friend?"

I glare at him. "I doubt he'd ask for five million in cash." I jut my chin towards the bag at my feet. "Besides, do you really think Lucifer would be so fucking cryptic about it?"

Damian stares at the bag for a moment, and the crease deepens between his eyes.

"Lucifer would make me squirm," I say, because that's exactly what the bastard was doing.

Damian meets my gaze and lets out a small laugh. "Yeah, he'd do more than just send a picture of her," he says and guilt bites at the lining of my stomach.

Before either of us can say anything else, our names are called, and we cross to the sleek jet sitting on the tarmac.

"My name is Josh and I'll be your pilot today. Unfortunately, because of the short notice, we don't have a stewardess for this flight," a young pilot I've never seen says to us. "I'm told they can squeak us in for takeoff in ten minutes. We should arrive in Athens just before seven p.m. Athen's time."

"Thanks," I say and take his offered hand.

"I understand the turnaround time may be quick?"

"That's what we are hoping. We will know more once we are on the ground and get our next set of instructions."

He gives me a nod and I take a seat, stowing the duffel bag under my seat instead of in the overhead compartment.

Damian slides into the seat across from me.

"Is that really five million?" he asks, pointing at the bag.

I roll my eyes. "What do you think?"

Damian smirks. "I think it's probably the petty cash in our safe and a whole lot of shredded paper."

I keep his gaze and cannot help the smirk that surfaces. He's only known me for six years, but he probably knows me just as well as CJ. A pang of sorrow hits deep within me. This will be the last time we work as a team. If I fail, I'll be the one to die today, but if I succeed, I'll never see my friend again.

I turn my gaze out the window as we begin our taxi out on the runway and focus on something else. If I don't watch it, he will sense the lies I'm feeding him, so I go over what happened with Bridget yesterday in as much Technicolor detail as I can muster. It's my buffer, my subterfuge while I figure out just what the hell I'm going to do once we are on the ground.

"You slept with Bridget?" His tone carries the shock displayed on his features.

"Yeah," I confirm, and look back out the window as we ascend into the clouds.

"What the hell were you thinking?"

I glance at him, unsure whether to be glad he took the bait of my surface thoughts or not. The one thing CJ and Steve taught me over the years was how to hide my thoughts when I really wanted to. If I concentrated on certain memories, I could think on a deeper level that they couldn't access. "I wasn't *thinking* at all," I say. "At least not with my brain, and I don't know what the hell I'm going to say to her when I get back."

"You realize she has a thing for you," he says and crosses his arms.

"She has memories of sleeping with me in high school, and a promise to her dead uncle to look out for me. That's not a thing."

Damian laughs, long and loud. "You don't know shit about women."

"I don't know. We had just gotten back from a job..."

"Wait. You took her on a job?"

"Yes. It was a ghost thing, and she can see them, too. I thought it would be helpful, but it turned out to be a disaster." I open that part of my memory, pushing it to the forefront of my mind, allowing Damian access to that piece.

He scrutinizes it, biting his lower lip as he assesses the situation, weighing each action and reaction in his mind. The open view layers another slice of guilt. When my phone buzzes, I'm glad for the diversion from his clinical assessment of my failure.

I glance at the sender and the message preview.

Bridget.

I sigh and open the text. The time blinks at the top, showing the same number as on the piece of paper in the envelope.

*We need to talk...*

"Yeah, I know." I can't help the verbal response and I look out the window for a minute, sharing the information with Damian without saying a word.

"See," he says, and I don't appreciate it. "And as far as bringing her in on jobs, she might actually be an asset to the company," he adds, yanking my attention back to him. "She didn't freak out. And she can see ghosts just like you."

"Yeah, but she could have gotten hurt," I say, and his eyebrows slowly rise.

"You have a thing for her?"

"No. Of course not. I just don't want to see her get hurt." I wave it away, and glance down at the text again, scrolling to see if she had any more to say. My brain jumps to the way she tasted as I stare at the next directive from Lucifer. The fact he is using Bridget's phone number does not sit well, either. It means he knows she isn't just another fuck.

When we land, a driver will be waiting and will bring us to where he has Hannah. Once inside, I am the one to deliver Damian's beating heart to Lucifer in exchange for my daughter. My stomach rolls, and I glance at Damian.

He's studying me, still lamenting on my relationship with Bridget.

"It's too soon." The words escape, wrapped in the anguish pummeling my insides. I can't hide the surfacing of emotion, and I use Raven's death as the buffer to the pain tearing me from the inside out.

Lucifer expects *me* to kill Damian.

How the fuck can I do that?

My eyes close and my head dips in defeat.

Damian mistakes it for grief, and his hand lands on my shoulder.

"What would Raven want?"

My throat constricts, and I slowly shake my head. *Get your fucking shit together. Hannah's life depends on it.* My silent admonishment comes from deep within the barrier, blocking Damian from any of the turmoil pounding my intestines to pulp.

"She would want me to be happy," I whisper, and force myself to look up through a sheen of gloss. When I blink, a hot path traces my cheeks. "But I just can't…"

He turns to look out the window. "I'm not one to talk. It took me twenty-five hundred years to let my guard down after Athena."

"Timing is everything," I mutter. "I gotta hit the head," I say, and unhook my seatbelt. I cross to the bathroom and close the door, just in time for my stomach to shoot the meager contents into the toilet. I flush and rinse my mouth out in the sink. With my stomach empty, I pull out the phone and stare at the response.

With a few keystrokes, I send another text, this time to myself from an unassigned number with the pickup instructions only and delete the item from my sent list once it is received.

I pocket the phone and wash my hands, avoiding looking at my reflection until I have finished. Silently, I reason with myself, trying to justify the horror I'm hours away from doing. There is no justification that will wipe away the building self-hatred, and I wonder if this is another step in tearing me down.

The sick truth is, I can't gamble Hannah's life on phantom intent. I have to follow the facts. Lucifer outlined a deal and CJ once told me Lucifer would honor the deal, although if there was a loophole in that deal, the devil would exploit it.

Is there a loophole here? One that I could capitalize on?

I can't think of one that would leave both my daughter and my best friend alive.

"Fuck."

I turn away from my accusing eyes and stomp back into the cabin, dumping myself into the seat. Digging in my pocket, I pull up the text I sent as the smoke and mirrors of the deal.

"I guess a driver will be at the airport."

His eyebrows rose.

"Yeah. I was hoping for an address and not this."
I run my hand through my hair, trying to think of
an alternate plan that would make us arrive at the
same place at the same time. "You have to figure
out a way to follow us," I say when I look back at
him.

He smiles. "It will be dark out, right?"

"I think it will be dusk, not quite dark," I say
because I don't think seven o'clock is after dark. If
it is, I've missed my first directive and Hannah will
suffer.

"Shit," he mutters. "I'll figure something out."

"Cab?"

The look he delivers tells me that is highly
unlikely.

"You're going to steal a car?" I ask in
exasperation.

The way he huffs at me burns, because when I
was in high school, I thought nothing of lifting a car
for a joy ride, but the last thing we needed was him
getting thrown in jail in a foreign country.

"I'm not going to get caught."

"Famous last words," I can't help the irritation.
"And what happens if you do?"

He sends that smile that leaves me uncomfortable. "Then I'll take to the skies."

"If you screw this up..." I trail off and close my eyes, leaning back in the seat. Damian wasn't the screw up on the team. I am. I have always been the one who is in the wrong place at the wrong time, and I pray this time, luck turns in my favor.

"I won't screw it up. I will be there to storm the castle with you, okay?"

I give him a nod.

"One more thing. Prepare yourself to take someone out."

The intensity of his stare makes me shift in the seat. He reminds me of my father. God knows I loved the man, but his moral compass was fucked up. Taking a life was easy when he thought it was warranted, but for me, it's much more difficult, even when it is warranted.

I'm not sure my soul will survive murder, but if it means my daughter lives, I'll yank Damian's beating heart from his body without a second thought.

I stare into the eyes of the man I have to kill in less than three hours and nod.

# Chapter 14

THE PLANE LANDS AND I grab the bag under the seat and take a deep breath. There is no way to be ready for this, and I send Damian a nerve-filled smile.

"If shit gets fucked up..."

"It won't. I'll be there. I promise." Damian unhooks his seatbelt. "Let me go first. That way I can scope things out and I won't lose you anywhere. Give me a five-minute lead."

I nod and remain in the seat while Damian climbs down the stairs. Josh glances in my direction.

"Sir?"

"I'm letting him scope things out." I get to my feet and cross to where he stands by the door. I glance out directly at the molasses colored sky and the sun low on the horizon, but at least it is still above the line. I made it here in time.

A measure of relief scrapes my back, but it is short-lived. Each minute that passes takes me closer to becoming a monster. I refocus on Josh. "The minute I get back, we need to haul ass home, no questions asked, okay?"

"Yes, sir. Mr. Beaumont was very specific with his directions."

"Ted's a good man." I glance at my watch. Almost five minutes have passed. "If we are not back in three hours, leave without us," I add and descend the stairs without a look back.

The walk into the hangar feels like everything is in slow motion. My examination of my surroundings doesn't reveal any danger, and I send my mental sniffer out looking for the same thing.

Nothing, except Damian's cursory inspection as well.

When I step through the doors, my scan passes over Damian at the phone charging stations. To the right of the charging stations stands a cluster of chauffeurs holding signs. The third one back holds my name and I cross directly to him, meeting his gaze.

"I'm Tom Ryan," I say.

"Do you have identification?" he asks with a heavy Greek accent.

I sling the duffel bag over my shoulder and scan his mind, just as Damian is doing. This man is just a hired driver, he knows nothing, and I dig in my back pocket for my wallet while trading a glance with Damian.

The driver studies my license and then gives me a nod. Instead of my back pocket, I stow the wallet in the inside pocket of my jacket. The driver's eyes widen at the flash of black metal and I stare him down.

"Astynomia?" he asks quietly as his eyes dart around.

I offer a tilted smile and put my finger to my lips. I'd rather have him think I'm a cop of some sort than a killer, and my actions seem to settle his nerves.

He turns and I follow to a stretch limousine, and he holds the door for me. It's the only stretch limo in the vicinity. Damian will have no trouble following this. The driver climbs into the seat and closes the divider. As he moves into the line of traffic, I glance back in time to see Damian slide into the driver's seat of an idling car.

His smooth exit into traffic makes me sigh and I turn towards the front of the car.

Another text comes through, and I again focus on Bridget and our little excursion last night.

"Alone?"

"Yes. Damian is following." I hit send and the television screen turns on in front of me.

When Lucifer fills the screen, every muscle clenches, and I wonder if I can follow the connection. The thought is dashed by the reality. If I leave my body for any reason, he has an opening to take possession. From the smirk on his lips, he knows that fact as well.

"You don't want to make the jump?" the teasing tone clenches my teeth and I shake my head. "Pity."

I keep my mouth closed because if I speak, I will issue every creative death threat I can think of.

"I have to admit, I was hoping you would not make it here before nightfall. I have been refraining from taking another drink from your daughter's potent blood," he says and steps aside.

Hannah is there, but she is hanging upside down in the same position I found her in July. Although the drip from her neck does not look like anything is flowing, unlike the river of red that flowed through the crude tube stuck in her before. Her terrified eyes meet mine through the screen and tears slide up her forehead and into her hair.

"Daddy," she cries.

"You son of a bitch," I growl, turning back to Lucifer.

"I have not turned the drip on," he says. "I trust Damian is close by?"

"Yes," I say, through clenched teeth. My fists are so tight I think my skin might split.

He just smiles and gives me an encouraging nod. With a flick of his wrist, the valve opens and a slow red flow fills the tube. "Just in case you have second thoughts. You now have less than an hour before she is drained of blood. The minute I have that little shit's heart in my hand, I will stop the drain."

The screen goes black, and my heart is throbbing in my chest, fear and desperation fight in every cell, and I knock on the window.

The panel comes down.

"How long until we get to our destination?"

The driver points to his GPS. "Twenty minutes if traffic cooperates."

I can't wait twenty minutes. "Can you go faster? It's an emergency."

He waves at the thick traffic ahead of us and I press my lips together.

*We need to get there within fifteen minutes*, I transmit the thought to Damian. *That's when our window closes.*

*So, clear the way. I'll keep up.*

I concentrate and floor the gas pedal under the driver's foot. He lets out a surprised squeak and presses on the brake. Nothing happens and I innocently ask, "Is everything okay?"

"No, sir," he says and concentrates on driving, although his heart is beating hard enough that I can see his temple throbbing.

I control the car's swerve between traffic, moving drivers out of the way if they don't yield to our fast approach, and catching Damian's car hot on our trail. The GPS beeps, indicating a right turn, and we take it, cutting off the line of traffic, and I keep the path open for Damian.

We are out of the city and winding into the green country. The GPS shows us minutes away from our destination, but I don't see any buildings, only a hill to our right and nothing but rolling fields in front of us. The driver takes the right and I get a glimpse of the city, before we circle around the base and slow to a stop in the hill's shadow. The structure in front of us leaves me speechless. The driver is panting, and brakes squeal behind us, jerking his head towards the rearview mirror.

"I apologize for my erratic driving," he says and slides out of the car. A moment later, he opens the door for me, and I tentatively step out with the duffel bag on my shoulder. My brain is skipping around and I give him a nod.

"Thank you. You are welcome to leave now."

"Oh, no, sir, I am supposed to wait for my next assignment."

"Leave," I order, and his eyes widen as he obeys the direct order. I step to the side of the road and Damian parks next to me, turning the car off before stepping out.

I wait until the taillights are gone before I focus on the house in front of us. My palms sweat, and I'm having a hard time drawing air; but I force myself to appear calm, even calculated.

"Let's do this." I take a step towards the house, and he grabs my arm.

Damian is scanning the modern design of the house, along with the surrounding area like he's trying to place it.

"I have less than five minutes to show up, Damian."

"I don't think Hannah is there. I can't feel her."

"I can," I say, and I'm not lying. I feel her getting weaker, but her terror is there, like a live wire. I'm surprised he can't feel it. "She's in there. Follow me," I say, and instead of sneaking in, I walk towards the front door. After all, in my bullshit story, they are expecting me and my bag of money.

The minute we clear the door, metal drops behind us, locking us inside. When the panel at the far end rises, my heart squeezes. Hannah is in the center, the line of blood filling a jug, like in every nightmare I've had since July. Her eyes widen at the sight of me.

I concentrate and close my eyes.

"What the…"

That's the last thing Damian says before I blow a hole in his chest. I spin and stick my hand through his shattered ribs, meeting his shocked gaze. My fingers grasp his warm heart and I yank, ripping it from its place before Damian can react.

Betrayal glazes his eyes, and I think I whisper I'm sorry.

I turn back towards my daughter and the devil standing next to her. The muscle still beats in my hand, spilling blood over my arm, and it runs hot on my skin. If I give this to Lucifer, both Hannah and I are as good as dead.

"Don't," Damian's last word pierces my ears just before his body hits the ground, and tears blur my vision.

His death plea doesn't make going through with this any easier. Lucifer starts in my direction and I know what I have to do. Before I can second guess my actions, I shove the entire heart into my mouth, crushing it to a pulp with my mind before forcing it down my throat.

From the surprise written in Lucifer's features, he never thought I'd pull a double cross, especially with my daughter's life in the balance. I had a moment to revel in the sheer bliss of fucking with the devil's plans before the power hits.

A bomb goes off inside me, shattering my cells from my stomach outward. I bellow with the pain of it. Everything Damian had, from the piece of CJ's power to the grace of Gabriel and Michael, slices through me. But it's Lucifer's grace that causes the agony. His grace not only fills me, it merges with my cells until every malignant force in my blood is boiling.

Lucifer is running in my direction, wearing a mask of rage. I roar at him. By sheer force of will, I pick him up and launch him towards the opposite wall. In the same moment, I vaporize Hannah's bonds and yank her towards me.

I miscalculate the distance between Lucifer and Hannah, and before I can react, Lucifer's sharp nails shred the side of my daughter's throat as they pass in the air. Her blood sprays and I am bellowing her name and sprinting towards her. She collides with my chest and I wrap her in my arms as her blood soaks through my shirt.

My gaze rises to Lucifer, climbing to his feet. The impact with the wall left crumbling drywall in his wake. My daughter's last gurgling breath pulls my gaze down to hers. The light fades from her eyes and my head whips back with the force of the cry ripping from my throat.

It swirls and ripples from me like a tornado, flashing red and black, as I hold my dead daughter to my chest. The ground rumbles beneath me and the only thought I have is to let it swallow me.

In the back of my mind, that little voice I hate tells me to get up and run. To get out before it's too late. I'm obeying, as the ground crumbles under my feet. With Hannah's body to my chest, I dodge from one crumbling strip to another until I'm beyond the kill zone. When I turn, I see rolling fire swirling, and blackened earth crumbles into the wide hole in the ground. Rage still shakes my form, and then everything flashes white, knocking me on my ass.

When the spots clear from my vision, I'm staring at a clear circle of dirt and Hannah's ghost standing in the aftermath. I have failed both her and Damian in ways I can't fathom, and I climb to my feet, focusing on my little girl.

If I can get her back to Valerie, she can be saved.

I reach out, grabbing Hannah's ghost before she can stop me. I'm in the stolen car before she can speak and I think I make it back to the terminal in ten minutes flat. With Hannah pressed to my chest and my hand tight around her ghost's wrist, I stalk to the plane, not letting anyone or anything deter me.

"Fly," I snap as I crumble in the chair.

When Josh doesn't move, I turn and glare at him. "Fly. Now," I say, and this seems to kick his ass in gear. He closes the hatch and disappears into the cockpit. Hannah's body has no warmth to it and she is hard to hold. She's dead weight, and it feels like I'm wrestling a rag doll. Her ghost is quiet, as she looks on with such sadness in her eyes that I feel the weight of my failure pressing down on my chest. I lay her body out on the chair across from me and kneel over her, pushing her hair out of her face. Unfortunately, I leave bloody streaks across her forehead.

"Just hold on, baby. It will be okay once we get home. Valerie will fix you up."

I don't know how long I kneel, running my hand through her knotted locks with one hand and a vice grip on her ghost with the other.

"Daddy, let go," her ghost whispers, and I look up at her.

"I can fix this," I say, refusing to let her go. Refusing to accept this outcome. I have damned my soul by murdering Damian, and if she doesn't survive this, there is nothing left.

"Daddy..."

"No, you listen to me! You are not going to die! Understand?" And with that statement, I push the plane into mach-speed. The sonic boom echoes through the cabin and the fuselage shakes against the knots I am forcing it to go. If it breaks apart and drops me into the ocean, I'm strangely okay with that as well.

Dying might stop the pain filling every cell of my being.

I go back to running my fingers through her hair, streaking it with her own tacky blood, but I'm too far gone to care.

The phone in my pocket buzzes and I let it ring. I don't want to lose physical contact with my daughter and I'm not letting go of her ghost, either.

I once forced my father's ghost back into his body, and I plan on doing the same once I get her to CJ's house. Valerie's healing power can fix this.

It had to.

The phone doesn't stop, and I finally untangle my fingers from Hannah's hair and pull the cell out of my pocket. Bridget's number flashes on the display and my fist clenches around the metal.

Lucifer.

I don't wait for his taunting. "I am going to kill you," I growl into the phone.

Silence.

"Tom?" Bridget's concerned voice whispers over the line.

I blink as my heart skips a beat.

"Bridget?" I'm unsure whether to believe it is her, or just another cruel joke.

"Damian's waiting at the office for you," she says in a soft whisper.

"Damian's dead," I say, and my voice cracks. Saying it aloud makes it real and my chest hitches. "I killed him, Bri," I add, using the name Hannah calls her. My head drops onto Hannah's stomach as I try to control the shaking overtaking my body.

"Yeah, I got that. He's pissed."

I huff. I can't blame him. I betrayed him on every level just to save my daughter.

"Do you have Hannah?" she asks.

I raise my head, scanning Hannah's prone form. "Yes, but I need to get to Valerie as soon as we land."

There is another pause on the line, and I hear something smash in the background.

"I think maybe I need to get out of here before he turns his anger on me," Bridget says.

"Tell him I'll be there soon enough, and instead of destroying the house you're living in, he can have a run at me."

I hear her relay the message, and the rumbling in the background continues until I hear a door slam.

"Do you need me to pick you up?" Bridget says into the phone.

I glance up at the ghost of my daughter and then her prone body. "Yes," I whisper. I can use all the help I can get right now, and I have a feeling after all this blows over, she will be the only one left still speaking to me.

That is, if Naomi doesn't tear me to pieces herself.

"Does anyone else know?" I ask.

Bridget laughs. "You and I are the only ghost whisperers in town, or haven't you figured that out yet?" The sarcasm in her voice rattles me.

I close my eyes and attempt to listen to what is going through her mind, but it's muddled. She's angry, disappointed, and hurt, but she also can't turn her back on the promise she made to her uncle.

"You should have told me," she says.

"If I told you, Damian would have known..."

She cuts me off. "You don't think he would have readily sacrificed himself for your daughter? Jesus, Tom, didn't you know how much he loved you? You were like a brother to him, and you pull this shit?"

Guilt and devastation mixes with the shakes already accosting me. I couldn't voice the remorse, it was just too big.

"I hope you know just how much you've fucked this one up," she mutters under her breath.

"I know, okay? I am painfully aware of how much I screwed this up," I yell into the phone. "Valerie can fix it. She can make things right. She has to." The rawness of my voice rings through the cabin and my vision blurs.

"Dad, you need to let go," Hannah says, and this time her voice sounds more mature.

I glance at her and shake my head. "Valerie will fix this."

We both look at her pale form that holds no hint of life, and I end the call with Bridget. I can't face more of her questions or accusations. Not when my little girl isn't breathing.

# Chapter 15

THE MINUTE THE PLANE lands, I collect Hannah in my arms and wait until Josh comes out of the cockpit. He leaves a wide berth, but opens the hatch and folds down the stairs, letting me exit without a word.

The moon has started its slow rise and I pause, staring at the fullness before I glance at Hannah's ghost, remembering my mission. People scatter as I enter the hangar, but I don't stop, not even when the security detail tries to change my course.

Nothing is going to keep me from getting my daughter's body into Valerie's healing hands.

Bridget steps inside just as I am crossing towards the door and her eyes widen at the sight of me. I get a glimpse of my reflection in the door behind her, and my forward motion stalls. I am drenched with blood. It streaks my exposed skin like some ancient Indian markings. Hannah is limp in my arms and she, too, is painted in deep red. The only clean one is the ghost whose wrist I grip with my free hand.

I resume my gait, crossing by Bridget without a word. The car waits at the curb, and I will the back door open, forcing Hannah's ghost in first before I climb in with her dead body.

It takes Bridget a minute before she slides into the driver's seat, and with shaking hands, turns the ignition. I don't speak. There isn't anything to say, but I avoid her glances in the rear-view mirror.

"Tom," she starts.

"Valerie can fix this," I say and finally meet her worried stare. "Just get me to CJ's house, okay?"

The minute we pull into the driveway, I'm out of the car, dragging Hannah's ghost along with me. I will the door open and march into the kitchen where everyone is congregating. Valerie is the first to see me and she gasps. The glass she holds tumbles to the floor, shattering.

I lay Hannah's body on the floor and slam her ghost down onto the prone form, looking up at Valerie. "Fix her," I growl.

Valerie's eyes bounce between my dead daughter and me, and then she is next to me on her knees with tears filling her eyes. Her hands float over my daughter's face and around the shredded bits that once was Hannah's throat.

"Fix her!" I yell in her face. "I have her spirit. I need you to fix her!"

When Valerie's eyes meet mine, I gulp down the fear, denying the truth in her gaze.

"Tom, I don't have the power to bring someone back to life," she says through a fog.

"Goddamnit, just fucking fix her!"

"Daddy, let me go," Hannah's ghost sobs as she struggles beneath my hand.

"Tom!" CJ yells, pulling my attention.

"Valerie can fix this," I insist and turn towards her. "Why won't you fix her?" I say, my voice filled with accusation and disbelief.

"Thomas Patrick Ryan!" a voice bellows from the family room. Her Irish brogue is unmistakable, and my gaze shoots to hers. Raven stands bathed in heavenly light, and I'm not the only one who can see her. "Let go of our daughter."

Her command falls between us and she blurs behind a flow of my tears.

"I can't," I whisper, and she moves forward, floating with grace I cherish. "You know damned well why I can't."

"I know. But you have to let her go, Tom," she says softly, her voice baptizing me in her disappointment.

"Please, fix her," I plea, turning to Valerie.

No one moves. Raven's hand reaches out and finds my cheek, turning my face to hers.

"Let me take her with me, Tom," she says ever so softly, and a sob escapes from my chest. "She deserves the peace of heaven."

I hang my head, knowing I'll never see either of them again. The peace of heaven is now beyond my reach. My punishment is just, and another sob breaks through my tightly pressed lips. I drag my hand away, releasing Hannah's spirit.

Hannah's ghost rises and places a soft kiss on my cheek before she takes her mother's hand and fades into the woodwork.

I shatter. There is nothing to hold me together anymore.

"Where's Damian?" Naomi's question breaks through my harsh sobs.

I don't look up at Naomi. I'm shaking too hard to function, but I squeeze out the words anyway because I owe it to him. I could coat it with excuses, with the promises Lucifer made, but that would cheapen it, make it less of the horrific act that it truly was.

"I killed him."

Silence surrounds me like a death march, and I slowly raise my head, meeting her horrified stare. Her mind becomes a flurry of questions, right alongside those accosting Valerie and CJ. It is only when Grace enters the room that their thoughts stop, and everyone focuses on my daughter's best friend.

She crosses the room slowly; her gaze locked on the dead body next to me. Tears brim, sliding down her cheeks as she slowly drops next to Hannah. Her little hands gently caress my daughter's cheeks and then she looks up at me with such pain that I gulp down my sobs.

"I forgive you," she says and I stumble backwards.

This child does not know what I've done.

"You stole my father's grace," she says, answering my thought. "And you did not give it to Lucifer." Her gaze drops to Hannah's dead form, and a tear slides down Grace's cheek, landing on my daughter's forehead.

I stare at the drop and then raise my gaze to Grace's.

"It still doesn't make it right," I say, despite my throat tightening. I force my gaze to the family surrounding me. Every one of them knows what stealing angel grace entails, and the disgust is written in their expression.

There is only one thing left for me to do, and I climb to my feet, navigating my way to the sliders. They open with no conscious direction and before CJ intercepts; I am sprinting towards the rock wall and the drop to the jagged boulders below.

I launch into a dive with my arms at my sides and I close my eyes, waiting for the impact. Air whistles in my ears and then a blow hits my midsection, driving me into a tumbling mass and I hit the frigid water twenty yards out from my original destination. The cold grips me and I surface, turning back towards the house. CJ stands at the wall with his fists clenched as tight as his jaw.

"You ain't dying yet," he growls low.

But this time, he has no control over me or my bleak fate. I close my eyes and stop treading water. I've never been a floater and without the motion of my arms and legs holding me up, I sink. While I want to die, it takes great effort to stop holding my breath and before I can suck in water, arms wrap around my neck, yanking me to the surface.

"Just as soon as I warm up, I'm going to kick your ass," CJ says to me.

"Just let me die," I whisper, trying to break his chokehold, but it's no use. He drags me to our dock and hauls me up onto the wood, where we both lay shivering.

I stare at the dark sky.

"I fucked up something fierce," I whisper.

He sits up and rubs his hands together, blowing on them to warm up before he looks at me. "When we fuck up, it's pretty damned colossal."

I let out a shocked laugh. Only my brother can make me laugh during the biggest tragedy of my life.

"Besides, I can't do this shit without you."

He concentrates on rubbing his hands together to warm them, and I'm still laying on the cold wood, hoping to freeze to death in the fall night air. Of course, it isn't even below freezing, so that's just wishful thinking on my part.

"I killed my family," I say and bite my lip. The fiery burn of tears blurs my vision.

"No. Lucifer killed your family."

"My actions killed them, CJ. I lost my wife because I said no to his offer, and my daughter because I didn't give him Damian's beating heart." I sit up. "I've got nothing left."

The left hook knocks me on my side and CJ glares at me. His silent rant is not so silent in my head and I rub my jaw.

"Like you wouldn't want to give up if you lost Valerie and Alex," I snarl, letting the anger overwhelm the self-pity. "Especially if it was because you fucked up."

CJ's glare remains but his rants soften.

"I murdered my best friend to save my daughter, and I couldn't even get that right." I let out a sarcastic laugh. "Lucifer is going to have an eternity with my ass. I'm sure it's going to be delightful."

CJ stares at me. "And you want to start paying right now?"

My first reaction is hell no, but that completely overshadows my will to die. I narrow my eyes at CJ. He brilliantly turned my death wish into the exact opposite, and I hate him for it.

"Fuck you," I mutter, because like it or not, while I don't feel worthy of living, I also don't want Lucifer to win at this shitty game. I climb to my feet and slick back my wet hair with my fingers.

"What would you have done?" I ask because I need to know just how off base I am.

CJ stares out at the water, weighing my question and he looks down at the wet boards beneath our feet before meeting my gaze.

"For my son," he says and presses his lips together, blinking away the sudden sheen over his eyes. "If there was a chance to save him, I would have done the same goddamned thing you did, with one exception." He looks over the water.

"What?" I can't read him at all and I'm expecting him to tell me he wouldn't kill Damian.

"I would have given Lucifer his grace," he says and turns, climbing up the stairs and leaving me with that morbid thought. He pauses and looks down. "In that way, you're a better man than I am."

His praise is unwarranted and I shake my head. "No, CJ. You've always been the better man."

He raises his gaze from mine, and he does a scan of the ocean, instead of addressing my comment.

As he turns away, I say, "I think I closed the portal." My brain is not entirely sure what the hell happened in Greece, but at some level, deep down inside where the angel grace rages, I know.

CJ's turns back towards me as he processes my words. His eyebrows rocket up and his jaw drops, making the look on his face that much more comical.

I huff a laugh. "I think I produced angel fire."

# Chapter 16

I FINALLY CLIMB UP and make my way into CJ's back yard. Bridget is the only one outside, and she sits on one of the lawn chairs waiting for me. I can't meet her gaze. Instead, I stare at the ground as I walk. To say I'm numb is an understatement.

She stands. "The police are here." She hooks her thumb over her shoulder.

I look inside. Bear is taking a statement from CJ, and he keeps glancing in my direction. I don't have an explanation. What I have is a pilot who saw me carry my dead child onto a plane in Greece, and a hanger full of people who saw me carrying her to the car here. And, of course, my psychotic rant for Valerie to fix her, followed by my suicide attempt. I wouldn't be surprised if I find myself in the psych ward on suicide watch tonight.

"I told them Hannah was kidnapped, you attempted to rescue her, and things didn't go as planned."

My eyes shift to hers and I give her a nod. "Thanks."

Bridget stares out at the ocean, avoiding my gaze. Her mind swirls with the loss of my daughter, and I blink at the pain centered in her aura. I didn't know she cared for Hannah that deeply.

When her eyes find mine, she asks, "Can I ask why?" She waves towards the rocks.

My eyes find my dripping shoes and I shake my head.

"You just have to concentrate on breathing; the pain will fade," she says.

My hands clench and I level a glare at her. "This differs from a car accident, Bri."

I know my words are harsh, but her loss was a tragic accident that had no bearing on a decision she made. She recoils and opens her mouth to speak.

"Do not compare my colossal fuck up to a car accident." I look back in the house as they place my daughter in a body bag. Just the sight of it washes the numbness away and clenches my insides with a pain right down to the cellular level. I close my eyes and turn away, ignoring the urge to pull the soaking revolver out of my holster to see if it still works.

"I made the wrong call," I say, and my voice is raspy, as if I've swallowed a bucket of glass. "I can't live with the results." I open my eyes and meet her gaze. "However, my brother, in all his wisdom, reminded me that if I put a bullet in my brain, Lucifer gets exactly what he wants. He gets me splayed out on a carving station for eternity." Tears burn the back of my throat and I find it difficult to swallow. "Whatever I do, I can't seem to win."

"Does it always have to be about winning?" she asks.

I stare at her. I want to ask what else there is, because right now I have nothing. "It's all I've got."

A throat clears and I turn towards Bear as he steps out on the patio with CJ.

"That envelope you got at the office. Do you still have the contents?"

I dig into my pocket and pull out the zip drive, tossing it to him. If the salt water hasn't corroded the disk, I'm sure I'll have more rigorous questioning soon, that is, if the content doesn't scare the piss out of him.

"Are these the terms of the ransom?"

I inhale. "Ransom. Okay, if that's really what you want to call it, then yes."

He studies the zip drive and then plugs it into the iPad he's holding. With a couple of swipes of his fingers, the screen fills with my daughter.

Lucifer's voice drives my teeth together in a clench, and I blink the edges of rage from my vision, choosing to watch CJ's similar reaction. Bridget stands, staring at the screen, her face bathed in horror, mirroring Bear's.

Bridget's face pales, and she glances at me with haunted eyes.

Bear's gaze jumps to mine as the video fades. "What the hell is that?"

"That is the thing that ordered my wife's death, and my daughter drained of blood. That is the fucker systematically killing off anyone who doesn't do his bidding." The words come out in a feral growl that Bear shrinks from. "That is the thing that waged war on us."

Anger rises to an uncontrollable level, but I'm helpless to stop it.

"*That* is the thing that killed my daughter, and I swear, as God as my witness, I am going to hunt him down and tear him into so many tiny fucking shreds, there won't be enough angel blood to rejuvenate that fucker."

Bridget's palm lands on my chest, and I look down at it. I hadn't realized I even moved from the space where I'd started, but I am now towering over Bear like he is a subject worthy of my wrath.

Bear's shaking hand is on his service revolver, and his eyes are wide and terrified.

When my gaze moves to CJ, his equally wide eyes shock me out of the fury burning my cells. The image he projects into my brain makes me stumble backwards and I trip, landing in one of the chaise lounges.

The mask of fury on my face was terrifying, especially since my irises looked like a fully involved forest fire. There wasn't a hint of my baby-blues in them and the kicker was the fucking massive midnight black wings that appeared out of fucking nowhere. The image is nothing like what CJ looks like wielding angel fire. His wings are as pristine white as the light in his eyes.

The image yanks at a memory and my stomach rolls. Before I can stop it, vomit covers the ground at my feet.

I look exactly like Lucifer did just before he killed my father.

# Chapter 17

I STAND UNDER THE hot spray of the shower at the cottage, trying to control the shivers knocking my teeth together. CJ took control of the situation as soon as I threw up. He palmed the drive and walked Bear around to the front of the house. I don't know if it was just CJ's influence or Bear's raw fear that concocted the lie about my daughter's death, but according to the coroner's report, as well as the news stories, Hannah died from a bear attack.

If I wasn't so fucking freaked out, I might find some irony and humor in the form of attack my ex-friend centered on.

Bridget helped me to the car and brought me here. I don't know if she is still in the living space or not. I just stand and let the burning water pelt my face and chest with no motivation to move. If I move, every horrifying thing that happened to me today will hammer my midsection like a prizefighter.

The door squeaks. I guess she didn't leave.

"Tom?"

I remain silent, but bow my head so the water flows down my back.

The shower curtain rattles enough so she can see I haven't done something drastic again. I turn my head and our eyes meet. I haven't said anything since we left the house. I have nothing to add.

When I lose my shit, I take on Lucifer's form and my angel fire is more like hell fire.

That makes me a world-class freak. Except Bridget isn't looking at me through that lens. I look away, because I can't deal with the awe living in her irises. I reach out and close the shower curtain.

She yanks it back open, this time wearing a glare, and she reaches out, turning the water off. "You're clean enough. Get out and get dressed." The bark in her voice startles me.

"Who the fuck do you think you are?"

"I'm the bitch who's going to keep you functioning until you can do it by yourself." She throws the towel at me. "Now move!"

Whether I want to, my body obeys because I'm too damned shocked at her little drill sergeant act to deny the orders. I stop at the sink to brush my teeth, because I still taste vomit and blood and need that final comfort before I can feel human again.

Clanking comes from the kitchen, and I wrap the towel around my waist, opting to see what she is up to before I head to the bedroom to find some clothes. She has the coffee pot brewing, and she catches sight of me out of the corner of her eye.

"What? You need help to dress now?"

"Cut the attitude," I snap back and her eyes narrow as her arms cross. "Fine," I mutter and turn. I avoid the second bedroom. Just passing draws a sharp breath and then I am past it and in my bedroom. I take a few minutes to pull on jeans and a sweater. I carry a pair of socks with me to the living area, dropping on the couch to slip them on.

As I sit up, she hands me a coffee. "I don't know if you need that or not, but it might help you warm up." This time, her voice is softer. "You still have a ghost to confront."

"I know."

"And you're stalling while he is probably ripping that house to shreds."

"It's all about you, isn't it?" I mutter under my breath.

"Sometimes it has to be." She turns away and collects her cup off the table.

I stare out the window, thinking about what Damian said to me on the plane.

"Bri, I'm damaged goods," I say, and I'm not sure why my throat tightens. I clear it, keeping my gaze outside, on the deep dark of the ocean.

"When did you decide to start calling me Bri?"

I shrug. "It's what Hannah said you preferred."

Silence, and then a sniffle comes from her direction and I turn. My jaw tightens as Bridget sits with her hair shrouding her face. Her shoulders shake in that all too familiar posture of sorrow. I know I should console her. Instead; I turn back to the window.

"I'm ready to go get my ass kicked." I set the coffee cup on the table and stand, crossing to the shoe rack by the door. My choices are limited to flip-flops or sneakers. "Where are my boots?"

"Everything you had on is in the dumpster." She stands and wipes at her cheeks before she meets my gaze. "I got the stuff from the pockets before I chucked it all," she says and tosses me my wallet.

Overshadowed with anger and disappointment, Bridget's soft nature is now creating hardness I never would have thought possible. She keeps my gaze as she passes me until she reaches for the doorknob.

I put my hand on her arm, because under all this badassery, she is hurting.

She stiffens at my touch and this time; she doesn't look at me, but she trembles under my fingers. I force her to turn, and then I pull her into a hug. I'm not sure why I do it, because solace is not what I want right now. I want to wallow in the pain until it swallows me and I disappear.

But she needs this.

From me.

And I can't deny her right now.

She folds into herself, and the tremors turn to sobs against my chest. I hold her, but I've got no more tears, and I've got zero in the way of reassuring words.

# Chapter 18

WE STAND IN FRONT of the door to our office and her apartment above. Smashing glass resounds inside; I take a breath and reach for the doorknob, stepping inside. Bridget doesn't make it through the door before it slams shut. The force rattles the molding, and it shakes the floor under my feet.

Bridget pounds on the door, crying out my name, but I'm too preoccupied with the destruction spread before me. Every stitch of furniture in the entryway is destroyed to the point the wood is in splinters. Glass litters the floor, and the same destruction is happening in my office.

"Damian!" I bellow, and the air stills.

The crunch of glass under foot announces his progression into the entry, and when Damian's ghost steps through the doorway, I actually gulp at his murderous gaze. Then again, I deserve every ounce of pain he intends to dish out.

I move into the middle of the room and open my arms wide. "Do what you have to do."

He charges, knocking me off my feet and into the drywall on the far side of the room. The impact pulls all the air from my lungs and leaves my ears ringing. His fist drives what little air is left from inside me, and the pain spreads, acute and welcomed.

After a few punches, Damian's ghost steps back, glaring at me. I lean against the wall, forcing my knees to lock so I don't slide to the ground.

"Fight back," he growls.

"No," I say in barely a wheeze. His fist connects with my jaw, and I stumble a few steps to my side.

"You fucking murdered me!"

I meet his angry gaze and nod. "Yes."

"Why?" he bellows and takes another shot.

I go down to my knee. The side of my face pounds with the pain. "Because that's what I had to do to get Hannah back alive. Your heart was the ransom." I force myself to look up at him and climb to my feet.

His eyes narrow. "Did you get Hannah back alive?"

My gaze drops and I shake my head.

"Then what the fuck did you kill me for?" His voice barrels out, rattling the windowpanes.

I shrink away from his anger. "What choice did I have?" I mutter and force myself to stand up straight and own the mistakes I made. "If I didn't bring you to him, he would have killed Hannah the same way he murdered Raven."

Damian loses some of his fury and his fists drop to his sides. The rage over this entire situation surfaces and I step toe-to-toe with the ghost, leveling my glare.

"Could you sentence your daughter to that kind of death?" I scream in his face. "So, yeah, I traded your life for hers and then I made a fucking mistake and my daughter died because of it."

His expression hardens. "The mistake you made was killing me!" He roars and throws his next punch.

I parry, blocking it, but I'm not fast enough to account for his counterattack. I sail through the air and land on my back in the center of the room. Before I can get my bearings, he's on me, lifting me by the throat.

I claw at his grip, trying to break his hold, but with my feet dangling above the floor, I have no maneuverability. He means to kill me, and CJ's words from earlier light a fire under my ass. I mentally push.

Damian's ghost loses his grip and falls back a few steps, and I'm once again on my feet, drawing in air in great gulps. When his fist connects again, the bone in my cheek gives and pain wraps all the way around my head until all I see are spots.

"Stop!" Bridget's voice cuts through the haze, and my triple vision slowly rights from my position on the floor. She stands between Damian's ghost and me, blocking him from delivering any more crushing punches.

His angry mask sets my heart on overdrive. It's one thing to let him pummel the shit out of me, it's another to let him harm her, but I'm too slow. His backhand sends her tumbling towards the wall.

I'm on my feet, and the fury inside me ignites, making every agonizing bruise he delivered fade to nothing. I roar at him, sending him crashing through the wall into his office. Drywall sprinkles the space, and he steps back into view, dusting himself off.

"You do not lay a hand on her," I growl, and point towards Bridget.

His gaze transitions from me to Bridget climbing to her feet, and the violent interest in his eyes has me stepping into the path between them.

"Don't you dare." My skin burns and my fingernails dig into the palm of my hands. The shift in the air is subtle, but it's enough to identify what's happening. The same sensation filled me when I lost it in front of Bear.

Damian stumbles back a step and grabs for the wall, the fire leaving his eyes at the sight of my transformation.

"You said yes?" he whispered, his ghostly eyes going wide with fright.

"No. This is what that bastard's grace does to me," I growl and point at him. A swirl of angel fire flies from the tip of my finger and wraps around his midsection, leaving just enough of a charred burn to make my point before I close my fist, making it disappear.

It takes Damian's ghost a full minute to digest the words, and the fact I could have toasted him with angel fire had I wanted to.

"You?"

His expression turns incredulous, like, I wouldn't have the guts, or the stomach, to eat a human heart, and it just fans the flames of irritation within me.

"Yes. Me." I stare at him, taking a deep breath, calming the burn back down; and rub my sore jaw, wincing as my fingers brush my broken cheekbone. "I heard you, and for once in my life, I listened."

"Are you two done destroying the place?" Bridget says from behind me, reminding us there is someone else in the room.

I meet Damian's gaze. "I'm sorry," I say, knowing it's not enough, and the hardness returns to his glare.

His internal fight with the fury bludgeoning him is written on his features. When his hands curl into fists, Bridget has her answer. He is far from done with me.

"Go upstairs, Bri," I say over my shoulder. I don't want her in the middle of this fight. Not when things were going to get bloody.

"Bullshit," she snaps, again stepping between us, her gaze bouncing between me and the barely contained rage across the room. "I'm not letting him kill you," she adds, staring me down.

She turns to Damian. "I'm not," she says, much softer and lowers her arms, shifting her stance into a defensive form. "So, if that's what you truly want to do, then you'll have to go through me."

I've never seen a ghost blink in confusion, but Damian does. The slow shake of his head worries me.

"You really need to be careful who you side with. He'll rip your heart out," he says jutting his chin in my direction. "Literally."

Bridget's serious expression alters in slow motion. The smirk finally appears just before her snort of a laugh. "Did you really just say that?"

I glance at her before looking at Damian again. His lips twitch and one of his shoulder's rises and falls.

"Put yourself in his shoes," she adds, after her snorting laugh fades.

"I would have told him what Lucifer was demanding," he starts, but Bridget's shift and crossed arms silence him.

"And then what?"

His mouth opened and shut a couple of times before he huffed and looked at the floor. "I would have found another way, and my daughter would be alive."

"Like Athena?" I say.

"I beat Lucifer before," he growls. "And I'll beat you, too."

Before I can blink, he has me pinned on the wall to my office, one hand squeezing my throat and the other aimed at my chest. My heart.

I close my eyes, expecting ripping pain, instead, his frustrated growl yanks them open again. His hand cannot pierce my skin. It can't puncture Raven's pendant.

"If I can't have your heart, no one else can," he hisses and tosses me across the room.

I laugh, flashing back to another time, and another ghost and within a blink, I'm pinned against another wall.

"I think Tanya said those same exact words." I squeeze out between hysterical laughter.

His angry gaze meets mine and I can't stop laughing. There's no rhyme or reason to it, either. I'm not sure if I'm having a bona fide breakdown, or what, but I cannot stop.

His grip on my throat loosens, and he actually glances back at Bridget before focusing on me again. "I meant..."

The start of his clarification just pushed me into the gale realm, and my knees buckled. He releases his grip, and I drop to the floor, holding my abdomen, still in hysterics until I fold over, pressing my forehead into the debris on the floor and shake until the laughter turns into something else entirely.

Laughter, tears, screams; I have no idea how to control whatever this is that grips me.

Damian retreats a few steps.

The flurry of emotions beating me to shit turns into a tornado, decimating everything inside me.

A warm hand lands on my back and the crunch of shifting glass settles next to me. Bridget's soft coo fills my world. Tones follow, like she's dialing, but I still can't stop.

"Hello, this is Bridget O'Keefe. I need an ambulance sent to 375 River Road."

Her words compute, but I still can't stop whatever it is that is happening. My insides feel as though they are shattering, and the shards are stabbing through every organ in my body, except my heart.

My heart continues to beat, to keep me alive, despite the pain.

# Chapter 19

I WAKE, GROGGY, AND my hand lifts to wipe my face, but stops with a clink of metal on metal. My gaze travels above me, focusing on an intravenous bag hanging on a T hook.

Scraping pulls my attention to the left and my stomach drops. Steve takes a seat in the chair next to me. His face was haggard and his eyes streaked with red veins. I glance around the hospital room and then at the wrist restraints, and back to Steve.

"Suicide watch?" I ask, because I know where I am.

Bridget covered up the destruction of the office by telling the paramedics I was responsible. They had to give me a sedative to get me to move from my balled position. I vaguely remember someone saying I was bleeding, and then the sweet bliss of nothingness.

"Yeah. Your prognosis is a tossup between psychotic break, or just a run-of-the-mill breakdown." He lets out a tired laugh. "Valerie came in and checked your injuries at my request," he added and folded his hands together so tightly his knuckles turned white. "Which might be why you are coherent now."

"How long have I been out?"

"They brought you in last night." He stands and steps to the small window. "CJ called me after you left the house." Steve's voice cracks, and his chin drops to his chest when he looks my way. A layer of tears coat his eyes. "I know how it feels to lose a child," he says and presses his lips together. "The only thing worse is the loss of a grandchild." He turns back to the window.

My mind fills with excuse after excuse, and I know they don't amount to anything. "I fucked up."

"I'd say so."

"How's Naomi?"

He stares at me and lets out a sardonic laugh. "How the fuck do you think she is?" His anger and disappointment lace his voice.

If I could shrink to nothing, I would. It was like asking me the day after Raven died how I was doing and I close my eyes, knowing it was an asinine question, but it popped out on its own. Now I'm afraid to open my mouth for fear of what other stupid questions might make an appearance. I don't know what else to say.

Strained silence settles between us, and I shift on the bed, trying to find a comfortable position.

"Is Bridget okay?" I ask, hoping the change in subject will warm up the chill in the room.

"She's been waiting for you to wake up." He crosses to the door. "I need some air anyway," he says and steps out of the room, holding the door for her.

When the door latches, Bridget crosses soundlessly and takes a seat. She glances at the bindings strapping me to the bed.

"You know, there was a time I dreamed of a situation like this," she says and her eyes meet mine. The smile on her face is framed with sadness.

"And now?"

"Now I just want to beat the crap out of you for so many things."

"Oh." I can't say I blame her.

"But I also want to be there for you. To help you get through this."

"You should run, Bri. Run far and run fast," I say and I mean it.

She runs her finger over the back of my hand. It's such a small gesture and yet says more than her words did.

"Don't fall in love with me."

Her eyes lock with mine. "It's a little late for that."

My eyes close and my head falls back on the pillow.

"Damian warned me about you when I started working at the firm. I guess he didn't realize I was already a notch on your bedpost."

"He knew." I meet her gaze.

She inhales and crosses her arms. "Just shut up and let me get this shit out."

"Fine." I really don't want to hear her out. What I want are no complications that Lucifer can exploit.

"He warned me that falling in love with you would be easy. That you are innately good and pure, right down to your core." She lets out a small laugh. "And it would be years before you let anyone else in."

I look up at the ceiling.

"I had no intention of opening my heart again, either. And then you were such a terrific dad." A tremor shakes her voice and I clench my teeth. "Everything he said that first day before you came into the office, he reiterated last night when I was cleaning up the house."

I turn, shocked by her words.

"That's how I know he wasn't just feeding me a line that first day." She sniffles and blinks her eyes clear. Taking a deep breath, she continues. "He may have wanted to kill you for what you did, but it was because he cared so deeply for you and your family."

"I'm pretty sure he wanted to kill me because I ripped his heart out with the intention of giving it to Lucifer," I say.

She does that half shrug thing and I can't tell if there is truth to my statement or not.

"Your little reveal about what exactly was at stake sank in after you left." She glanced away from me. "He also muttered something about some twenty-five hundred odd years was long enough. What did he mean by that?"

"Damian Andreas was born in 500 BC."

She laughs and I remain stoic. When I don't change expression, her laugh fades.

"You really believe that?"

I look down at the binding holding my wrist. It unlocks, and I signal her to move closer. She gives me a skeptical look, but scootches forward in the chair. I move the wisps of her bangs to the side and place my palm on her forehead. With a breath, I transmit the total of Damian's life into her brain. Everything from his first memory to his last. I had every piece ingrained.

I knew how he felt about my brother and me. None of his thoughts, feelings, or experiences while he was breathing was a mystery, but his response as a ghost—that humbled me.

The transfer took moments, but when my hand relinquishes her forehead, I act on impulse, running my hand into her hair and I pull her to my lips, because I know after seeing my ultimate act of betrayal, she will never forgive me.

She fights against me at first, but after a whine of derision, she melts into the kiss and our tongues slowly twirl. The kiss consumes me, showing me the possibility, and with it, the need to burn this bridge before something horrifying happens to her. Finally, I release her before I end up pulling her onto the bed with me.

Bridget puts her forehead on mine for a minute, closing her eyes. "Damn you," she whispers, just before she pulls away. Pain resides in her hazel eyes, along with a thin sheen of tears.

"I'm sorry. I know I shouldn't have, but..." I quietly trail off and drop my hand into the restraint, willing it back in place.

She gives me a little smile and takes a minute to smooth her hair back and gather her wits. It was quite the opposite of her uncle's reaction when I downloaded Damian's life to him. "There was one more thing Damian wanted me to tell you." She draws a deep breath and sighs.

I wait for her to form the words, wondering just how long they'd talked.

"He said, since you seem to have such a mastery over angel fire, you need to be the one to close the portals."

"I don't even know if it is angel fire." I say, but my argument is based on self-doubt, not the facts, not the certainty present in my heart.

"He thought you might say that," she says and smiles. "But he assured me that was angel fire, and from what I saw CJ do, I would have to agree. Damian really knew you better than I think you know yourself."

I let a light laugh escape and turn my gaze to the ceiling. "Damian only saw what I wanted him to see. He never saw any of the darkness. Raven didn't see it either, but it's there, poisoning everything that once was good in me, and I'm afraid I might not be able to contain it anymore." I have no idea why I'm confessing this to Bridget, but it's tumbling out like I've been given a dose of truth serum. "And there's a part of me that doesn't want to contain it. It's like the part of me that wants you in my life, despite the odds of you becoming a target." I huff. "But I know better now."

Silence blankets us, and I keep staring, waiting for her to speak. I finally glance at her and see tears slowly tracking down her cheeks. My hands ball into fists as I resist the urge to wrap my arms around her.

"I should have said no to you when you asked for a job. That would have been the best way to protect you." I let out a sarcastic laugh. "I was so damned naïve."

"Damian said CJ would not close the portals. He won't leave his family. Not unless he is forced to." Her voice cracks as she tries to get the conversation back to what Damian wanted, and not what either of us might want. "He said that's what you needed to do to keep *his* family safe. He said you owed him that much."

I close my eyes against the burn of tears and turn my head towards the tiny window. She's right of course. I owe Damian this, even if it means I never set foot back in York, it's the only way to keep what's left of both our families alive.

I nod, with my eyes still closed.

"I'm coming with you."

My eyes fly open and my head snaps in her direction. "No fucking way."

Her low chuckle catches me off guard. "I've got nothing left here, either, Tom. At least if I'm with you, I can help. I can make a difference."

"Did you not see what I'm going up against? I'm not bringing you anywhere near that." My heart pounds against my chest at the thought, but her eyes are unyielding, taking on that drill sergeant quality again.

"Bri," I start and take a deep breath because now my chest is tightening with the start of a panic attack. "You give him leverage."

Her eyebrow rises.

"I give a damn about you, okay?" I snap.

"I give a damn about you, too." She crosses her arms and cocks her head as if to say take that. It's adorable and clouds my thinking.

I lay my head back on the pillow. "I can't take you with me." I don't leave room for negotiation in my tone. If she comes with me, it will be a disaster of epic proportion.

# Chapter 20

THE HOSPITAL IS VERY serious about their thirty-six hour suicide watch, but at least after the first twenty-four hours, they take off the restraints. I appeased the resident psychiatrist, and he signs my release form on the third day and hands me a counseling schedule for the next month.

I stare at the paper showing three sessions a week and balk.

"I really don't need this many sessions," I say, holding up the paper.

Dr. Minswell just raises an eyebrow.

"Fine," I answer and fold up the paper, stuffing it in the pants Bridget brought this morning. I climb down the stairs and step out into the crisp autumn air.

She pulls my car up to the curb and gets out, tossing the keys to me without a word before climbing into the passenger side. I feel as though I'm going from one psych ward to another, but I climb into the driver's seat.

"I'll drop you off at the office. I need to take a drive."

"I'm good," she says.

"I'm not going to off myself," I snap and send a glare at her.

"Fine, then you won't mind if I tag along."

"Jesus Christ, woman, can't I have a couple of hours of peace?"

"What are you doing?" she asks, challenging me.

"Planning my daughter's funeral."

Her cocky, overbearing attitude disappears. "Oh. Okay. I'm sorry."

I sigh. "I know you mean well, but you can't be my shadow. Not today. Today, I need my time with my little girl, okay?" I glance at her and she nods. "So, the office?"

She gives me a small nod.

"I'll be a couple of hours. You have my cell if you need me," I say as I pull up in front of the house.

She pauses. "Are you sure you don't need me?"

I give her a soft smile. "You'd know if I needed you." If my day goes as I expect, I might just need an ear when I get back. I made an appointment with the funeral home, but that isn't scheduled until late this afternoon.

This morning, I have a completely different destination. I was serious about time with my little girl and the only place that can happen now is Paradise Cove.

Bridget stops at the door and glances at me. I give her a half-hearted wave and back out of the driveway. I head in the opposite direction of York Village. The drive to Brooksfield is only an hour, and I have time to mull over what I'm going to say to my wife.

I cross over the frost-ridden grass to the path leading to Paradise Cove, still unsure of what I want to say. Her disappointment in me was pretty clear the night she took Hannah to heaven. I slow to a stop before I cross onto the soft moss.

The person standing with her back to me is not who I expect. The minute I step onto the moss, my mother turns towards me.

"They thought you would come sooner," she says and turns back to the sun dancing on the water.

I give a nervous laugh. "I would have, had I been able to. They had me on a thirty-six-hour lockdown."

She glances over her shoulder with a crease between her eyes.

"Suicide watch," I admit, and heated shame fills my cheeks.

"Tom," she sighs, and there is sadness in her eyes that chokes me.

"I know. I've gotten lecture after lecture about the sanctity of life, over the last three days." I can't stand having my mother look at me that way. It's almost as if I've already been lost to her. "Can I talk to my wife and daughter?"

Her gaze drops to the ground. "It's not sanctioned."

"Sanctioned? What the fuck does that mean?"

"It means you are damned," she says, turning in my direction. "And there are major... discussions going on upstairs as to what that means."

I stare at her, waiting for more, and she crosses to me.

"They can't come. If they did, it would upset things more than they already are."

"But, Mom," I start and she shakes her head.

"I may have already done irreparable harm to your case by coming." She closes her eyes. "But I couldn't leave you here thinking we all abandoned you. We are trying." Her hand caresses my cheek.

"I still don't understand." I can feel the tremble in my lips.

"The argument to set aside your damnation is raging. It's ugly and heartbreaking."

I hang my head. "I guess Damian would lead the opposition."

She hooks her finger under my chin and raises my face so I meet her gaze. "He is fighting for you. Every life you ever touched is fighting for you. Raphael is even fighting for your redemption."

"Dad was forgiven for all the shit he did. And if Damian is up there, he was forgiven for his sins, too. Why is my head on the chopping block?" Aggravation fills me.

Her fingers caress my cheek. "You betrayed and murdered someone who loved and trusted you. It's the ultimate sin."

"So, I should have let Lucifer torture Hannah? Kill her?"

"There is no justification for what you did, Tom. The ends do not justify the means."

The snap in her voice stings because I know she is right.

"So, basically heaven is closed to me, along with whatever magic this cove offers."

She bites her lip and nods.

"And there is nothing I can do to change it?" I ask, because without hope, I am lost.

She closes her eyes, and when she opens them; I have my answer. Tears brim, sliding down her cheeks.

I step back. "So, my options are close all the portals and try to stop the devil from getting hold of Naomi and Grace, in exchange for an eternity being ripped to pieces over and over again, or say yes to Lucifer and become his weapon and possibly survive eternity without torture?" My voice rises with anguish and anger.

"No. Those aren't your only choices. You can help close the portals and let us hash this out, knowing every portal you shut down is a step closer to us." Her snarling reprimand makes me feel like a little kid. "Don't you ever contemplate saying yes, do you hear me?"

She blurs through my tears and hot trails slide down my cheeks. "I won't."

"Promise me," she insists.

I look up at the sky and then out over the mountains on the other side of the lake. The need to never disappoint my mother again outweighs my hesitation. Despite that, the words stick in my throat. When I bring my gaze back to my mother, I force the words out.

"I promise," I whisper with a quivering voice.

My chest squeezes when she fades away.

With that promise, I have damned myself in other ways.

Lucifer won't ever give up his quest to tear me down, and anyone I care about will be at his disposal.

# Chapter 21

I WENT DIRECTLY TO the funeral home after leaving Paradise Cove, instead of waiting for my original meeting time. My instructions are simple. Cremation and no service. I will handle the service myself. Hannah will get the same treatment Raven did.

"When can I have her ashes?"

"Friday. Do you have an urn picked out?"

I shake my head and he guides me to the adjoining room displaying coffins and a mantle with various urns. One has blue butterflies painted on it and I bite my lower lip, pointing at it.

"She'd love that one." My voice is raw, and he gives my shoulder a caring pat.

"I'm sure she would."

I take leave and head over to the office. I haven't been inside since the night Hannah died, and I wonder how far in the cleanup Bridget really got. When I open the door, fresh paint assaults my nose and I scan the pristine entry. Even the drywall is fixed. A radio blares from my office and I step to the doorway.

All the debris is gone, and Bridget is erasing the damage with a fresh coat of paint. With her back to me, she wiggles to the music as the roller drifts up and down the wall in a uniform strip. Her hair is piled in a mess on her head, with a random streak of paint on the side, like she swept a stray wisp away without the knowledge her hand had paint on it. The entire effect is so sexy and down to earth that the overwhelming need to strip her down and ruin her paint job takes hold.

I take a step into the room and stop. The promise I made to my mother makes this impossible, and I turn away, crossing to Damian's office instead. His office is still furnished, and everything is mostly untouched.

I take a seat in his chair and stare at the pictures on his desk. Naomi and the kids stare back at me with beaming smiles. Guilt edges in and when I turn to the other photo on the desk, my hands grip the chair arms. It's a picture of me and Damian holding up a fifty-pound striper and grinning like fools. The fact that the picture sits on his desk is like a kick in the gut.

It's funny. In all the years we've worked together, I've never noticed the pictures on his desk or the stupid little knickknacks on his shelves. Things representative of his current life. Things I'll miss like fishing with him. That damned fish fed our families for months.

The hole in the center of my chest grows with each memory. When I finally look up, Bridget is in the doorway with the paint roller dangling from her hand.

"I didn't hear you come in."

I just shake my head. "Sorry."

She disappears, but before I can get to my feet, she is back, wiping her hands on a cloth and crossing to stand at my side.

"Are you okay?"

I stare at the picture, wondering if I'll ever be okay again. I look up at her, and my need burns through every caution flag in my brain. The small shake of my head sets her in action. Bridget pulls me from the seat and into her arms in a warm hug.

My arms wrap around her, holding on as tightly as I dare. I hadn't realized I was trembling until she grounds me in place. We stay like this for a while and then she makes the mistake of looking up at me. Tears cluster on her eyelashes and sparkle in her eyes.

Her hand snakes to the back of my head, and she pulls me to her lips before I can break the hold. The moment the kiss ignites, I turn with her in my arms and press her to the wall, following my base instincts and not what my head is telling me.

At the core, I need human contact. I need to feel adored. I need heat and passion, and everything that makes life worth living. Without it, there is nothing left to fight for.

The kiss breaks, and her aura flares iridescent pink. She takes my hand and leads me up to the bedroom, and I let her, despite the objections in my head.

In the confines of her bedroom, she focuses on unbuttoning my shirt in silence. I pull the elastic from her hair, freeing her messy blonde locks. Her hair is like silk on my fingers, and I slowly comb through it with my fingers. When she winces, I meet her gaze, catching the flare of pain in her eyes as I extract my fingers from the knot. The small rush of air between her lips calls my attention and when her tongue wets them, I can't help myself.

Holding her face, I lean in, delivering a kiss along with every bit of my fractured soul. I want her to understand everything, and I pull her to me, deepening the kiss as she whines under the intensity of it. Every thought, every memory, every emotion running through my form flows into her.

Wetness flows over my nose and I don't know if it's her tears or mine. What I shared with Raven was a fraction of what I am downloading into Bridget. This hides nothing, it bares all, right down to the petty jealousy I harbor for CJ.

It isn't a matter of love or trust. This is an act of desperation. I need to know that someone is capable of loving me, even after I show my darkest secrets. When the last memory transfers, the last moment before this second, I break the kiss and step away. Her eyes slowly open and focus on me as if she's seeing me for the first time.

Her aura flares like the sun for a moment, and then threads of iridescent pink weave through it, along with deeper pink and blue.

"You really are beautiful," I whisper with a sigh and meet her gaze.

She doesn't move or respond just yet, and an icy fear grips me. It must show on my face because she quickly shakes her head and closes the gap between us, taking both my hands in hers.

"I'm not rejecting you. I'm just... processing everything." She keeps her eyes locked on mine and releases my hands. I can't see a hint of pity in her eyes, just a combination of heat and sadness. Her hands move up my chest until her palm stops right over my heart. Her lips twitch into a smile. "Your heart feels like a jackhammer."

I allow a smile. "Yeah, well, I just pretty much bared my soul. Even the shitty side of it that no one has ever gotten a glimpse into."

"You've been through a lot of dark times," she says.

I narrow my eyes at her. "You're not... freaked out?"

"No. I've skated on the dark side myself, so I'm not one to judge. Of course, I never killed my best friend..."

She pulls the hand that isn't over my heart away from my chest and shrugs with it. I can't tell if it's a dig or a half-assed attempt at a joke, and I'm not sure how to respond.

"It changes nothing." Her soft affirmation rocks me to the core.

"You still want..." I can't finish, and I press my lips together against the rest of the question and the turmoil her words cause inside me.

She doesn't answer, instead; she steps closer, pressing her lips to my chest. When her kisses trail lower, I close my eyes and tilt my head back, letting an inaudible sigh, framed with her nickname, roll from my tongue.

I remember what Bridget O'Keefe can do with her mouth, and she is just as skilled, and twice as sexy, as she ever was in high school. The low hum in the back of her throat nearly does me in and she goes deeper, swallowing me until her lips caress my balls.

"Oh. Fuck." I groan, unable to hold on any longer. I come in her mouth, and she sucks until

I'm trembling. "Okay." I whisper, and she rolls her tongue around the sensitive tip before leaning back on her heels.

Her hazel eyes are almost entirely green and her aura pulses in time with my cock. I can hardly keep my balance, but I help her to her feet and lead her to the bed in the corner. This time, I'm not frantic, like I was in the kitchen. This time I linger, memorizing the sensations of my mouth on her body, her soft skin under my fingertips, every physical contact between us until she is trembling beneath me as badly as I am.

I climb back to her lips, and deliver a sensual kiss that locks a rumbling moan in both our throats, and then I pull away, searching her eyes.

"You didn't happen to pick up anything since the other night?" I ask, poised in place, aching to feel her pussy wrapped around me.

The ecstasy etched on her face fades and her eyes close. "Shit."

I roll onto my back and stare at the ceiling. Silence falls with only our labored breathing to voice our mutual frustration.

"Fuck it," she says and swings her leg over me, sliding my throbbing cock inside her before I can stop her.

The moment her hips start that slow grinding circle, my reservations fade, and I close my eyes, savoring the sensation. I make a mental note to keep my head this time, and pull out before I shoot my load.

When I open my eyes, I take her in, from her bright aura, to her messy blonde hair and hazel-green eyes. Her summer tan still hangs on and the bikini patches on her breasts show me just how skimpy her summer attire really is.

As my gaze scans her, I zero in on a small tattoo that I missed the other night, and again tonight. I'm not sure how I missed it, considering how fully I explored her, but right next to my thumb, just below her hip bone, are three small hearts and one heart is new. I run my thumb over them and glance up at her.

Her hips still and she glances at where my thumb is, and then lets out a soft sigh. "A heart for each lost child," she says, and her cheeks redden in embarrassment.

"This one is new." I lightly pass over the raised skin with my finger.

Her hips slowly twirl, and she leans forward, kissing me instead of answering. Mingled with the kiss comes her memory. My little girl captured her heart, and the tattoo was Bridget's way of dealing with her death. It's a mark to remember her by, to honor her spirit, just like the other two honor her own children.

I deepen the kiss, sliding one hand in her hair and the other cups her ass. The rawness of her emotions ensnares me, and I can't stop. I need more, more of her heart, her mind, her gentle soul.

Her hips speed up, riding hard as her teeth clink mine. We shift, deepening the kiss until I am overwhelmed with stimulus. I siphon every memory she has, collecting them, storing her lifetime alongside those that mean the world to me.

Her moan fills my mouth as her body tightens and her orgasm milks me, clenching and unclenching around my cock with such intensity it drives me right over the edge. When our lips unlock, she pulls up for breath and her bright eyes stare into mine.

Both our chests heave and she has a light layer of sweat that makes her skin glisten. I want to lick her all over again.

"I felt you," she whispers.

I let out a sharp laugh. "I would hope so," I say, because to me, my come must have felt like a fucking rocket.

Bridget rolls her eyes. "No, well, yeah, I felt that, too. But I'm talking about you being inside my head. I felt you there." She bites her lower lip as her thoughts swirl around my words more than hers, and then her head drops to my shoulder. "I meant to stop before..."

So had I, but I got so lost in the feel of her and the feed of her memories, that I just plain lost my good sense, which seems to be the pattern here. I stare at the ceiling, unmotivated to move, wondering why I keep letting this happen.

"I meant to as well," I admit with a sigh and lock eyes with her.

"We can't keep doing this," she says and rolls off, snuggling in the crook of my arm.

"No shit."

She glances up at me and concern floods her gaze.

"We need to make sure we have protection next time," I clarify, and the worry lines on her forehead smooth. She lays her head back on my shoulder.

"Nice save there," she mumbles, and I give her a soft squeeze.

I smile, but as her breathing smooths out into a light snore, my smile fades. This is all wrong, and my eyes close at my utter stupidity. I'm not sure if this is a half-assed attempt at saying goodbye or just a selfish act meant to reinforce my broken ego before I go hunting for Lucifer's portals.

Bridget's utter acceptance of me clouds my judgment. It doesn't hurt that she's sexier than hell and actually has a good heart, despite whatever misgivings I had about her in high school. She had been part of the bitch squad and I assumed she belonged there, just like I had assumed Raven was an outcast who wasn't worth the hit to my social status before I really got to know her.

I stare out at the darkening skies, wondering what would have happened if I had seen under Bridget's facade in high school. I glance down at her and shiver. An odd certainty grips me. If I had taken a deeper look, I would never have given Raven a second glance.

The ramifications of not having Raven in my life play across the shadows on the ceiling. The Windwalker might not have been caught. Steve's FBI career would not have been cut short. Valerie would have died at Damian's hands. CJ probably would have gone dark. And the most significant ramification, I would not be suffering with the loss of my wife and child. I wouldn't be fraught with fear at the very thought of trying to build something with Bridget.

# Chapter 22

TWILIGHT MOVES INTO NIGHT and I continue to stare at the shadows, measuring my next move. Sometime over the past couple of hours, her light snore transitioned to the deep cadence of sleep, and I make a decision.

I slide my arm from under her. She rolls and curls into a ball. Before the chill wakes her, I cover her with a blanket, and climb out of bed as soundlessly as I can.

She stirs, but I will her to remain asleep.

My clothing is scattered, and I dress in pieces until I'm completely covered. I pause at the door and take one last look at her before slipping out of the room. I head down to the office where my indiscretion started, and pull a couple of pieces of paper out of the desk's top drawer, along with a pen.

The first note isn't long. It is to CJ asking him to take care of Hannah's remains, and when my house is done, to rent it out so it isn't empty for however long I'm gone. He'll understand; if not, I'm sure I'll get a flood of texts and phone calls.

The next note is harder to write, and I close my eyes, clenching the pen in my hand before I attempt to explain.

*Dear Bri,*

*I have no excuse for what I'm about to do, at least one that you'll ever forgive me for. You really should have heeded Damian's warning. I seem to make a habit of tearing hearts out, and I'm sure you'll damn me all to hell after this, but I have to go.*

*I have to try to redeem myself before I have any hope of a happy ending.*

*For what it's worth, right now, that happy ending includes you, but I know once you read this, that will no longer be possible.*

*I need to close those portals. It's dangerous and I have no idea if I'll ever get back home. I don't expect someone as beautiful as you to wait around for a damned jackass like me, but if the fates see fit, maybe we'll find each other again.*

*Know that tonight will be a lifeline for me. The one thing that will keep me moving forward, even when I want to lie down and die. The memory is cherished enough in my heart to do that. So, yeah, I kind of give a damn about you... a lot more than I should.*

*Thank you for sharing your soul, and I'm sorry I have to break your heart.*

*Tom.*

I stare at the words and leave the paper on the desk before crossing to the bookshelf. The map Damian and I made showing every conceivable portal in the world is folded neatly between Shakespeare and Stephen King, and I pull it from its place.

I hesitate at the office door and turn back, grabbing the photo of us with the fish. It's a heavy reminder of what I owe him, and I'm sure there will be days I need the reminder. I open the closet door and exhale. This space was left untouched by Damian's rage and I squat, unzipping Raven's duffel bag, and stow both the picture and map on top of her crystals and potions.

My leather jacket hangs untouched, and I slip it on, picking up the bag before I make a last sweep of the empty space. I haul it over my shoulder and head for the front door. My hand reaches for the doorknob, but I hesitate, my chin dropping to my chest as new loneliness layers over my own shattered heart.

I pull my hand back and glance at Damian's office before I cross and scribble a postscript on Bridget's note.

*PS... you can stay as long as you'd like and run the business while I'm gone. I'll make sure you have whatever you need.*

It isn't much, but at least she won't have to figure out money or housing on top of losing a piece of her heart. I walk out without another glance and climb into my car, even as my heart and mind continue to argue over this decision.

The lights are still off in the bedroom, and I back out of the driveway with only my fog lights on. At the cottage, I throw the few articles of clothing and toiletries that I have into a bag, and I'm in the car in less than ten minutes.

I don't have a plan beyond heading west. There are twelve remaining portals in the western hemisphere, stretching from Alaska to Argentina. We mapped another twenty-five overseas, covering every continent on the globe except for Antarctica, which seems to be free of any portal and angel kin alike.

I glance at the European map, staring at the number of portals in Greece. The cluster is bigger than the one that had resided in New England and a shiver crawls through me.

Greece is my end game. Just like York is Lucifer's. But for now, the nearest portal is in Detroit, so that is where my redemption starts.


The End


Continue reading Tom's story with Angel Fury.

# About J.E. Taylor

J.E. Taylor is a USA Today bestselling author, a publisher, an editor, a manuscript formatter, a mother, a wife, a business analyst, and a Supernatural fangirl. Not necessarily in that order. She first sat down to seriously write in February of 2007 after her daughter asked:

> "Mom, if you could do anything, what would you do?"

From that moment on, she hasn't looked back.

Besides being co-owner of Novel Concept Publishing, Ms. Taylor also moonlights as a Senior Editor of Allegory E-zine, an online venue for Science Fiction, Fantasy and Horror, and co-host of the popular YouTube talk show Spilling Ink.

She lives in New Hampshire with her husband and during the summer months enjoys her weekends on the shore in southern Maine.

Visit her at www.jetaylor75.com to check out her other titles.

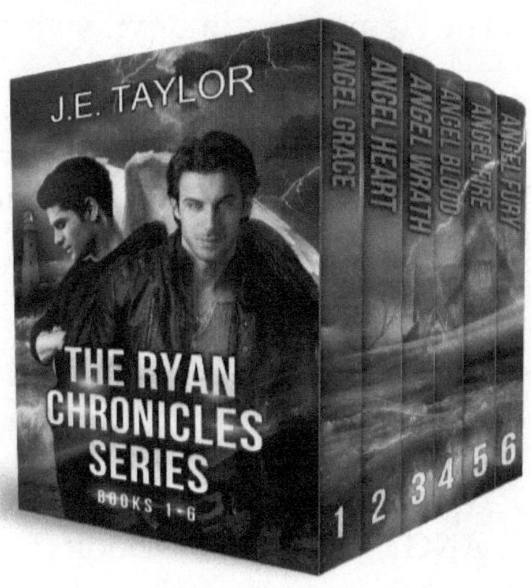


# THE RYAN CHRONICLES

**Demons, vampires, angels, and the devil.
What the hell kind of nightmare do I live in?**

CJ Ryan was born with enough psychic power to destroy the earth. And Lucifer wants him to do just that.

Raised with a strong moral compass, CJ won't sacrifice innocent lives to protect his own, and that puts him at odds with the devil.

But if he doesn't give in, he and all he loves will become the target of Lucifer's rage.

When CJ gives his twin brother, Tom, a dose of his powers to keep him safe, it puts Tom directly in Lucifer's crosshairs.

As the final battle draws near, what will they have to sacrifice to keep their loved ones safe?

Can they survive the devil's wrath?


THE RYAN CHRONICLES includes these titles:

CJ's Story:

ANGEL GRACE - Book 1

ANGEL HEART - Book 2

ANGEL WRATH – Book 3

Tom's Story:

ANGEL BLOOD - Book 4

ANGEL FIRE - Book 5

ANGEL FURY – Book 6


Fans of Supernatural and Shadowhunters will enjoy this series.

You might also like the GAMES THRILLER SERIES which highlights CJ and Tom's parents and their unorthodox history together.

# GAMES THRILLER SERIES

**Intensely disturbing. Beautifully horrific. Indescribably intense.**

When Ty Aris kidnaps Jessica Connor for his stepbrother's underground film network, he is not prepared for the impact she has on him.

His obsession with her lights a fire under his ass to get out of the ungodly business with his stepbrother.

But the only way to leave the business is in a body bag.

In the dark plane between life and death, Ty is given a choice: save his soulmate or save his very soul.

The Games Thriller Series includes:

Fallen – A Games Series Prequel

Survival Games

Mind Games

End Game

# THE STEVE WILLIAMS SERIES

Special Agent Steve Williams excels at his job, catching the most heinous of monsters walking the earth.

Serial killers.

When his job brings him face to face with a psychic, he struggles to accept her gifts in his neat little black and white world. Armed with her visions, along with his skills as an FBI agent, he hunts the worst of the worst, but will he catch the killer before they set their sights on him?

*Unstoppable, breath stealing, and terrifying all at once.*

*Gripping, rich and magnificent!*

The Steve Williams Series mixes compelling crime thrillers with supernatural forces that will grip the reader from page one. This six-book series takes you through some of Steve Williams' darkest cases in his FBI career.

The STEVE WILLIAMS SERIES includes Dark Reckoning, Vengeance, Hunting Season, Georgia Reign, Crystal Illusions, and Saving Face.

Find these titles and other fantasy and suspense titles on J.E. Taylor's website!

www.JETaylor75.com